THE
BONEMENDER'S CHOICE

THE
BONEMENDER'S CHOICE

HOLLY BENNETT

ORCA BOOK PUBLISHERS

Library and Archives Canada Cataloguing in Publication

Bennett, Holly, 1957-
The bonemender's choice / Holly Bennett.

ISBN 978-1-55143-718-7

I. Title.
PS8603.E5595B653 2007 jC813'.6 C2007-902361-4

Summary: In this third volume of the Bonemender series, Dominic's children are
kidnapped, but before they can be sold into slavery, a deadly plague strikes.

First published in the United States 2007

Library of Congress Control Number: 2007926215

Orca Book Publishers gratefully acknowledges the support for its publishing programs provided by the following agencies: the Government of Canada through the Book Publishing
Industry Development Program and the Canada Council for the Arts, and the Province
of British Columbia through the BC Arts Council and the Book Publishing Tax Credit.

Cover artwork, cover design, interior maps: Cathy Maclean
Typesetting: Christine Toller
Author photo: Wayne Eardley

The author is grateful for the support of the Canada Council
for the Arts which enabled the research for this book.

In Canada:
PO Box 5626, Stn. B
Victoria, BC   Canada
V8R 6S4

In the United States:
PO Box 468
Custer, WA USA
98240-0468

www.orcabook.com
Printed and bound in Canada.

Printed on 100% PCW recycled paper.

010 09 08 07 • 5 4 3 2 1

For Kate and Wally, who have cheered me on this adventure from my first hesitant steps, and provisioned me along the way with everything from pirate books to my very own tiny Elvish muse.

Acknowledgments

With the kind permission of the great Canadian musician and songwriter Willie P. Bennett, I have given a couplet from his song "Brave Wings" to Féolan.

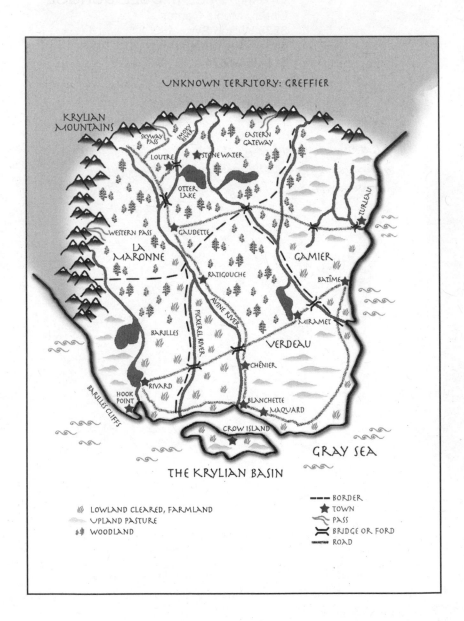

UNKNOWN TERRITORY: GREFFIER

KRYLIAN
MOUNTAINS

SKYWAY
PASS

SMOKY
RIVER

EASTERN
GATEWAY

LOUTRE

STONEWATER

OTTER
LAKE

TURLEAU

WESTERN PASS

GAUDETTE

LA
MARONNE

GAMIER

RATIGOUCHE

BATÎME

AVINE RIVER

BARILLES

PICKEREL RIVER

MIRAMET

VERDEAU

CHÊNIER

BARILLES CLIFFS

HOOK
POINT

RIVARD

BLANCHETTE

MAQUARD

CROW ISLAND

GRAY SEA

THE KRYLIAN BASIN

🌾 LOWLAND CLEARED, FARMLAND
⛰ UPLAND PASTURE
🌲 WOODLAND

--- BORDER
★ TOWN
〰 PASS
⌒ BRIDGE OR FORD
▬ ROAD

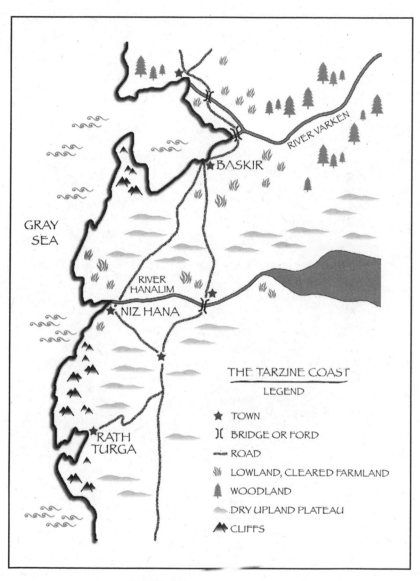

RIVER VARKEN

BASKIR

GRAY
SEA

RIVER
HANALIM

NIZ HANA

RATH
TURGA

THE TARZINE COAST

LEGEND

★ TOWN

)(BRIDGE OR FORD

— ROAD

🌿 LOWLAND, CLEARED FARMLAND

🌲 WOODLAND

DRY UPLAND PLATEAU

▲ CLIFFS

Note: These two maps are drawn to different scales.

CHAPTER ONE

GABRIELLE GAZED DOWN at the little village. It was just a handful of modest cabins, the farthest one a charred mess of caved-in blackened timbers. At least, she thought, the wind had been in their favor, and the fire had not spread to the other dwellings.

Jacques, Gabrielle's guide, had already ridden ahead, eager to arrive with his help. She hoped she *could* help. Burns were not only terribly painful, they were among the most difficult injuries to recover from. If she could save the girls—and by the guide's account, she was not certain she could—there was no telling what sort of life they would face.

As Cloud carried Gabrielle into the village, Jacques pointed her toward one of the little cabins. "Aline's waiting," he said. The door opened, and the woman ran to meet them, weepy with mingled hope and fear. Smudged still from the fire, hair mussed, she bore the hollow haunted look of new grief.

"Thank the gods you're here. My poor girlies. My poor little girlies!"

She stopped in front of a small cabin—"My mother's house," she explained—and paused in the doorway.

"I hope I haven't done wrong," she burst out. "Old Anna, that's my neighbor, she told me to coat 'em up in butter—"

"Tell me you didn't." The words were out before Gabrielle could stop them, and she rued her own brusqueness. The popular folk remedy was harmless enough on superficial burns, but with the injuries these children must have, it would be disaster. The thought of trying to clean rancid goat-butter from open wounds filled her with despair. But the last thing this woman needed was a scolding.

"I didn't," Aline said. "I couldn't bring meself to, on that raw terrible..." Again, sobs overtook her as she pushed open the door. "I just poured cool water over their little legs. It's all I could manage."

"You did exactly right!" said Gabrielle. "I couldn't ask for better." She laid a reassuring hand on the woman's shoulder and felt it slump with relief, but she didn't linger. With the opening of the door, her mind had veered mid-flight to the sounds coming from within. There was no screaming—not any longer—but rather a stream of hopeless gasping mews exhaled on every breath.

"They're quieter now," offered an older woman—Aline's mother, no doubt—from within the single room of the house. "The pain must be easing."

Gabrielle knew better. The pain would not be less—if anything, it would make itself felt more fiercely as the first shock wore off. The girls were simply exhausted, unable to summon more than this feeble expression of agony. She knelt beside the two small bodies that lay together, stomach-down, on a pallet in the middle of the house.

Gabrielle's eyes traveled over their light brown braids, pale freckled faces turned to each other, thin stick arms. Their eyes, dull with pain, were a matching hazel brown. Identical twins, they were, not more than four or five years old. The burn searing across the backs of their legs was a mess of red flesh and black char, but she knew she must leave it for now. First things first. Shock, lung damage, infection—any one of these could kill children so young.

Their pulse ran faint and rapid, their breathing the same. The airways, though, seemed fairly clear—only an occasional cough or raspy breath. They'd kept low to the ground, had perhaps been spared the worst of the smoke. Gabrielle laid a hand first on one thin back, then on the other, as she closed her eyes and let the world fade away. In the deep quiet she created around herself, the healing light kindled in her hands, and she went with it, sinking her awareness deep inside her patients. Yes, their lungs were doing fine. But the children's strength was nearly gone, seeping away with each panting breath. Deep in their chests, Gabrielle felt the twin hearts laboring too fast, too weak. The trauma, the pain, the terrible injury itself—it was too much for such small bodies to withstand. The girls wavered on the thin dividing line between life and death. Soon they would be beyond returning.

Gabrielle had been in that gray land herself. She knew it could be called a kindness to let the girls slip away, free of the pain and the fear. But she thought too of Aline's stricken careworn face, of the girls' father braving fire itself to save them. If she could bring them back, she would.

She sat up. "Aline? I need your help. Your mother's too."

The girls' grandmother was at her side already. "Anything. And call me Colette."

Gabrielle was checking the burn now. It was as deep and ugly as she had ever seen, eating in some places right through the skin into muscle tissue, but she saw cause for hope as well. The beam had fallen square across the girls' thighs, managing against all likelihood to miss both knee and hip joints. That would be a blessing if they managed to pull through.

"You've done a good job at rinsing off the wound," said Gabrielle, "but it needs to be cleaned more. You see here"—she pointed—"where a piece of nightgown has burned on, or here where the skin has made a blackened crust?" Her clear green eyes met Aline's fearful brown ones, held them steady. "These need to be pulled away. It won't be easy, and it will hurt your daughters. But if you can do this, then I can be working at the same time to strengthen them and help them to endure it, and they will have a better chance of living.

"I think," she added quietly, "that this may be their *only* chance of living. Can you do it?"

Aline's eyes flinched over the crusty surface of her daughters' legs. As if in anticipation, one little girl gave a sudden cry and thrashed feebly.

Aline glanced at her mother, pulled her mouth into a determined line and nodded. The older woman spoke for both: "Whatever's needed." Gabrielle pulled out her tweezers and scalpels and showed them how she wanted it done. Then she rummaged in her bag once more for the two big jars she had brought along for this very purpose.

"What's that, then?" asked Aline, a little suspiciously.

"This is honey," replied Gabrielle. "A treatment I learned from the Elves. It fights infection and seals over the wound to protect it. Much, much better than butter. When you have cleaned things up as best you can—you won't get everything, but try to clean away any charring bigger than, say, your fingernail—then I want you to drizzle the honey over the entire area. It will make a sticky mess, but I want every speck of that burn coated in honey."

"All right but…" Aline took a deep breath. "No offense to you, Lady, but I thought this is what you came here for? Will you not treat their wounds?"

"I will be treating their wounds from the inside," Gabrielle said. "I'm going to help their hearts to beat and their spirits to hold fast to the earth. It will look like I am asleep, but I will be working very hard to keep your girls alive. If you need me, call my name and I will awaken."

She expected—and got—the white-eyed, half-frightened look of wonder that came over the two women's faces. Until she had met the Elves, she was the only one she knew with this power to heal from within.

"What are your daughters' names?" she asked gently. If she needed to call to a fading soul, a name might make all the difference.

It was the grandmother who answered. "This one here is Mira, the other Marie."

Gabrielle had to smile. "All right then, we'll start with…"

She looked at the two small faces, alike as two chicks. How could she choose? While I help one, the other could slip away, she thought, and that was beyond bearing. She slipped her fingers around each girl's skinny wrist, counting first one heartbeat, then the other. The same.

In fact…She checked again. Yes, their heart rates were almost perfectly synchronized. She watched the girls' backs rise and fall, matching each other breath for breath. She caught her own breath in sudden excitement.

They were twins. As close to one body as you could get in two people. She would work on them both as one. If they were going to live, they would live together.

Gabrielle sat herself by the girls' heads and laid a hand on each neck.

"Give me time to strengthen them before you start—say a quarter-bell," she told her helpers. "Then get started." And she closed her eyes, summoned the light and allowed her mind to flow into two twin sisters named Mira and Marie.

CHAPTER TWO

ARS RINGING WITH the clash of his own hammer, sweat pouring down his bare chest from the fierce heat, Derkh was in a world to himself. He loved it when he got to make something that took real craftsmanship—something beyond the stirrups and horseshoes, plowshares and hoe ends that filled his days.

He had been working on this set of fine hunting knives—a short, back-curved skinning blade with a built-in gut hook and a long straight blade for killing and disjointing—for days now. Commissioned by a well-to-do sheep rancher for his son's fourteenth birthday, it was a job that, done right, could bring in more. Derkh meant to do it right.

He plunged the skinning knife, still red with heat, into the bucket. Water hissed and steam billowed. It was a little drama he had reenacted countless times, one he always enjoyed.

Only when he pulled the blade out and squinted along its length did he notice the woman.

Not that she was easy to miss. He remembered her instantly—she had served him ale at a local inn, and he had marked how she held herself like a queen despite her load of mugs and the foam dribbling down her arms.

She stood now in the entranceway to the smithy, watching him coolly. Bronze hair, tawny skin, amber eyes—if a gold statue came to life, Derkh thought, it would have her coloring. Then she walked—no, *prowled*—across the yard toward him, and any resemblance to a statue vanished. She was like a great tawny cat, lithe and beautiful and dangerous.

"Help you?" Derkh armed sweat from his forehead and tried to look self-assured.

She smiled, showing perfect white teeth. "You are young one. Is good."

"I'm sorry?" Her words were heavily accented, much stronger than his own telltale Greffaire overtones.

"Mistress say, deal with young one. Old smith is not much worth."

Derkh winced. It was true his master's work was becoming sloppy. His eyesight was not what it had been, nor his steadiness of hand. These days Derkh tried to steer Theo toward "minding the shop," but he wasn't always successful.

"What can I do for you?"

Again the smile. Gods, it was blinding.

"You can fix?" She held up a bridle, or rather a former bridle. Derkh took a look. Been left outside, by the looks of it. Half the bit and its hardware were rusted—that would have to be replaced. Couple of bridle rings too. The other side was fine though, and the leather just needed a good cleaning and oiling.

"Yes, of course," he replied. "It won't be that much cheaper than getting a whole new bridle though—I'll need to replace about half the fittings."

She shrugged. "They want to fix. Is not my say-so."

"All right. I can have it done tomorrow afternoon."

Business concluded, his self-consciousness returned. He felt naked, truth to tell, standing in front of this glory of a woman. It didn't help that he *was* half-naked, stripped to the waist but for the leather apron and forearm cuffs that provided some protection from the sparks that showered from his hammer.

He risked a glance. She hadn't moved.

"Is there something else?"

Those strange eyes pinned him. He had never seen eyes that color in all his life. They reminded him now of an eagle's, fierce and golden. He felt, fleetingly, like a raptor's prey before the strike.

"Your name."

"What?"

"Your name," she repeated impatiently. "What is name?"

"Oh, sorry. Derkh," he mumbled. Eternal night, you sound like a half-wit, he scolded himself. Speak up.

"My name is Derkh," he shouted. I *am* a half-wit, he despaired and gave up.

"I am Yolenka." Yolenka flashed him another brilliant smile, a smile to bless the entire earth and send a flash of heat right down to his toes. "I am happy to be meeting you."

YOLENKA RETURNED THE next afternoon to pick up the bridle, and later that week with a couple of saucepans needing new handles and again to pick them up. Each time she managed to arrive when Derkh was alone in the smithy, and each time she stayed longer than the time before. He began to get over his natural shyness and look forward to her visits. But it never occurred to him that she was actually interested in him until the night he found her waiting in front of the shop at the end of the day.

"You are finished with working?" she demanded.

"Yes," he agreed, wishing he'd washed up more thoroughly. He always rinsed off and stuck his head under Theo's pump before heading home, but only a proper bath could really wash away a day at the forge.

"I have night free also," she announced, with a delighted flash of teeth. "You eat with me!"

"HELLO, MY BEAUTY." Tristan's extravagant kisses—one for Rosalie, one for the gentle swell of belly where their third baby was growing—would have fooled almost anyone. They didn't fool her. His mind was somewhere else.

"What is it, Tris?"

Tristan, still wrapped about her middle, gave her a startled look and straightened. "Gods above, Rosie. I pray I never have some evil secret to keep from you. You are like a truth-sniffer from the old tales!"

Rosalie grinned, triumphant. "Well?"

"Well, I think I'd like to greet my wife and get all the way into my house before plunging into the news."

He got a little way in—as far as the first salon—before the interrogation continued. This time he didn't hide his concern.

"It's these raiders, Rosie. There's been another strike down the coast—that's three in a month, after such a long time with next to none. And it wasn't just a quick hit on the richest houses—they stripped Côte Noire village of every tool, coin and head of livestock to be found. I have a feeling we're heading into another spate of trouble, like Dominic had a few years before the war."

Tristan had fought in that brief war when Greffier, the

country north of the Krylian Mountains, had invaded the Krylian Basin seven years before. That event had forever separated his life into "before the war" and "after the war." Rosalie, though, had spent that year safely on the coast with her father. The war barely seemed real to her. Tarzine pirate raids, however, had been part of the backdrop of her childhood. Though the raiders had never been bold enough to raid the merchant warehouses at Blanchette, preferring the less rich but defenseless villages and towns nestled along the Verdeau coast, the threat of a pirate attack had been a favorite subject of conversation among the wealthy citizens who often sat at her father's table.

At the time, her father's assurances that the pirates would not harm *her* had been enough. Now Rosalie's heart went out to the villagers who had endured the terror of the attack and who might have lost loved ones as well as their means of livelihood.

"There must be some way to defend against them, Tris," she declared. "They cannot be allowed to waltz in here and help themselves whenever they wish!"

"My thoughts exactly, Rosie girl," said Tristan.

Three times a mother, she thought fondly, *and he still calls me his "girl."*

"We don't have the troops to fortify the entire coastline," he continued, "but there has to be some way…" His words were interrupted by the sound of small feet sprinting down the hallway, followed by a heavier tread and a reproving voice.

"Papa! I knew I heard you come home!" A small towheaded boy burst into the room and hurled himself into Tristan's lap as though for protection. He was followed by a breathless nurse with a curly-haired toddler on her hip.

"Now, Romy, I told you to wait—I'm sorry m'Lord. He got away from me."

"He's good at that, isn't he?" Tristan agreed with a grin. He ruffled the boy's hair, and five-year-old Jerome—named after his paternal grandfather, killed in that same war—smiled fetchingly at his nurse, certain now of his refuge.

"That's all right, Ginette. Leave the little monsters with us now." Two-year-old Aurele had already squirmed and fidgeted half out of his nurse's arms, and she set him down with relief.

"You shouldn't do that, Tris," Rosalie said, when the nurse had closed the door behind her.

"Do what?" Tristan raised innocent blue eyes to her, his leg never ceasing the violent mad-horse ride he was giving Romy, his voice pitched above the boy's excited squeals.

"Undermine poor Ginette like that. She has her hands full enough as it is, without you countermanding her orders every time the children manage to escape her."

CHAPTER THREE

ALINE TOOK A TENTATIVE hold of a black crust of nightgown with the tweezers and tugged. The charred cloth did not come free. She had to work at it as Gabrielle had shown her; and as the bonemender had predicted, water did not soften away the worst of the adhesions. The first time she used the knife was the worst. Mira's sudden cry of pain, the weak writhing of her legs as she squirmed to get away, brought the tears stinging to Aline's eyes. How could that woman have left her to do such a heartless job, and she a trained bonemender?

Her mother's gnarly fingers grasped her arm. Blinking to clear her vision, Aline turned to her mother. Colette thrust her prominent chin toward Gabrielle. The beautiful young bonemender's eyes were closed, her head bowed over the girls.

"She's an odd one, daughter, and no mistake. But she's the only bonemender we have, and the only chance we have. We have to trust her."

"I know it. You don't have to tell me." Aline's flare of anger brought her strength, and she made herself turn back to the grisly work. This time, she thought, the cutting brought a weaker reaction from her daughter, but whether because it pained her less or because her strength was on the wane she could not say.

Bit by bit, the larger pieces of crusted skin, cinder and cloth

were freed, leaving behind weepy raw flesh. The next step—
cleaning away the smaller crusts—would be a little easier, and
without any word spoken the two women sat back on their heels
with a sigh.

"I got the shakes," Aline confessed, holding out a trembling
hand. "I need a minute." She got to her feet, dippered water from
the iron kettle by the hearth, drank and splashed the remainder
over her face.

When she returned, her mother pointed her chin once more
at Gabrielle.

"Look at herself."

The bonemender was…panting, almost. As if she'd been running, or…Aline didn't know what.

"Is it a fit? What's wrong with her?"

Her mother shook her head, turning down the corners of her
heavy lips in an expression of bemused doubt.

"Blessed if I know. She'll have to look after herself though.
We need to finish up."

Aline turned back to the hateful task. Like peeling a burnt
potato, she thought, and was nearly sick as the image collided
with that of the girls as babies, chubby and smiley and with hair
like twin puffs of milkweed.

IT MUST BE because they were both outsiders, decided Derkh.
That was why Yolenka had sought out his friendship.

And that was, indeed, part of it. Derkh would have been
astonished to learn that Yolenka also found him attractive—his
pale skin, coal-black hair and broad chest almost as exotic to her
as her sinewy golden grace was to him. Besides, Derkh intrigued

her. There was more to him, she sensed, than a shy hardworking blacksmith. As there was more to her than a barmaid.

Derkh had long ago given up feeling he needed to hide his Greffaire past, but he was not a big talker and once the bare bones of his story were told—how he was injured nearly to death during the invasion battle, how Gabrielle saved him and brought him home with her—Yolenka had to probe for every additional detail. One fact impressed her more than anything.

"You know Elves!" she all but accused. "In all my traveling, I never see these people. I must meet!"

She had none of the Maronnais caution about new people and experiences, Derkh noted. Nor did she suffer from his own tongue-tied awkwardness. Her story tumbled out in a long stream of talk, helped along by several glasses of a fiery liquid she called *stitza*.

"I am dancer," she began. "Tarzine dancer from"—a grand wave, vaguely southward—"over the sea. I dance with great troupe, famous in my land. We come here, go to every country, kings' courts and biggest market cities. Is good here. They never see such dancing. The gold and silver comes in, is easy travel, no warlords. Riko is very happy."

"Riko?" Derkh ventured. Her man, he guessed gloomily.

"He is boss of our troupe. He run everything, say what we do."

"What do you mean, warlords?"

Golden eyes glared at him. "Is my story. I tell it. After will be time for warlords."

"Sorry."

Yolenka continued. "Tour is big success. Then in city called

Gaudette, king say, 'You go up to mountains where soldier camp is. Poor soldiers is bored, need a change'." She sniffed, offended still. "Like we are no more than a game of *reneñas*. Was insult. Still, Riko say we go—he wants king kept happy."

She meant the sentry force at the mouth of the Skyway Pass, Derkh assumed. There was a permanent camp there now, maintained ever since the Greffaire invasion. But with each passing year, a new attack seemed less likely and the size of the force dwindled. He could well believe the men posted there in the empty lands bordering the mountains at the northern edge of La Maronne were bored.

"So. Off to soldier camp, and we dance on bare ground not even combed smooth. I am waiting by side for my last"—she paused, searching for the Krylaise words—"well, there is big jump at the end, and as I am leaving a soldier reaches out for my sleeve and I am off my middle."

Balance, Derkh guessed she meant, but did not interrupt.

"And Gervil, my partner, is showing off to the woman he wants to take to his bed, and so when I am not just where I should be he is not noticing this, and he fails the catch and I fall."

Golden eyes rested on Derkh's face, eyes that knew bitterness but held not a shred of self-pity. Yolenka shrugged, a gesture that reminded Derkh of the flexing of great wings. A dancer. No wonder she was so...like she was.

"I know when I land I will not dance again," she said simply. "My knee was...*ffit.*" The plosive wordless sound said it all. "I come here, to Loutre, to be mended. The troupe goes home to Tarzine lands. I stay."

Derkh looked at Yolenka, confused. He had been drinking the

stitza as slowly as he could, but the stuff went straight to his head, and he wondered if he had missed something. The story seemed to be suddenly finished, but he didn't understand.

"But why did you stay? Why not go back home with your people? Your knee seems all right now." He remembered the first time she walked into the yard, the lithe power in her stride.

The shoulders flexed again. "You have not seen our dance. Is not just—" She rippled her body, a movement both languid and derisive. "Is full of leaps and"—she rotated a finger to show a spin or twirl—"at full run. I cannot do. So what then? Riko owns my work. What use is to him, a dancer with no jumps? And I do not want to be washing costumes and cookpots for troupe. Me—I was first of dancers! So. If I cannot dance, I am better living here. I look at my gold, offer Riko half to be free from him. He is happy to take it."

In the days that followed, Derkh and Yolenka learned more of each other's homelands. Both were harsher lands than the Krylian Basin countries, but the resemblance ended there. To Derkh, raised under the absolute, strictly ordered rule of an all-powerful emperor, Yolenka's portrait of a land where the king's authority was secure only in a few densely populated and prosperous pockets, where lawless warlords fought over the outlying territories, was baffling.

But her description of the warlords reminded Derkh where he had heard the word "Tarzine" before.

"I thought the Tarzines were pirates," he ventured. "At least I've heard of pirate raids on the coast here."

Yolenka's reaction was immediate and ferocious. "I know them. Turga's men." She spat, and not delicately. "Turga's land is small—he is squeezed between two strong warlords. So he claim the sea as his territory. Is pirate of Tarzine lands as much as yours."

GABRIELLE WAS BREATHING with the girls. Breath for breath, she
matched their rhythm as her heart beat faster than any resting
adult's should. She had never done this before, but she knew it was
working. She could not *give* them her air, but she could boost their
faltering efforts with her own strength and steadiness.

She wished she could take on the pain for them too, give
them even a brief respite. She felt the echoes of their anguish as
she worked and sent what strength she could spare to help them
endure the sharp tearing as the dead crusts were cut away. But she
was already spread so thin, working on two at once. Keeping them
alive was her first task, and after that only healing would bring
true relief from pain.

She knew when the worst of the cleaning was over, as she
knew when the honey oozed over the girls' ravaged legs. She knew
because she felt the changes in sensation as they gusted past her, but
the knowledge registered in some deep part of her mind beyond
words or thought. Her awareness was intent on keeping the tiny
engines of the twins' bodies running.

One bell, then two, passed. The small hearts beat more strongly,
and Gabrielle eased away from them, letting her own heart and
breath return to normal. She gulped deep delicious lungfuls of air,
relieved to see the girls holding steady on their own. Now she could
send all her energy into healing their wounds. Four small legs filled
with healing light as her mind coaxed the healthy flesh bordering
their wounds to grow faster than it ever had before.

CHAPTER FOUR

ELEVEN-YEAR-OLD MATTHIEU DesChênes sprinted along the narrow walkway that led from the mews to the scullery entrance of the castle and heaved open the oak door. Matthieu would have happily spent all day with the falconer had his tutor allowed it—there was a merlin in early moult, and a fierce new gyrfalcon being trained. But he had been given just a meagre dollop of free time at the end of the afternoon, and now he was late for dinner again and would be later still once he had cleaned up. Sneaking in the back way was only putting off the inevitable.

"Stars above, Master Matthieu, you look like something to be plucked and eaten, not a young lord heading to table."

Too much to hope he might escape Corinne's eye. He offered the head cook a sheepish grin, made a halfhearted effort to brush away some of the feathers and straw clinging to his jacket and dodged past her broad floury bulk through the scullery and into the servants' hallway. From there it was a quick dash up the back stairs and through the hallway to his chamber.

Matthieu pitied his sister Madeleine, who had turned thirteen last fall. She was "a young lady now," his mother said and had to eat with the adults at the royal table every evening. Matthieu was glad he still got to eat in the small dining room with his little brother

Sylvain and their nurse. Even after his birthday, just a few weeks away, he'd have a whole year of freedom from formal dinners.

At least most nights he would. At every moon-change—new, half and full—the family dined together. It was "good training," his mother said, and for those dinners he had to have clean clothes and proper manners.

Matthieu threw a fresh jacket over his questionable tunic—if it doesn't show, it doesn't count, he decided—and scrubbed his face and hands over the basin. A hasty rake-down of his brown hair and he was ready.

There were no guests, thank the gods. With a mumbled apology, Matthieu slipped into his seat, avoiding his mother's disapproving stare. Grandma Solange had been speaking when he arrived—that meant his parents would have to let her continue instead of giving him a lecture. Another piece of good luck.

Solange smiled at Matthieu, giving no sign of irritation. "I'm glad you're here, Matthieu. There is some news you will want to hear."

Now her smile encompassed the entire family—her oldest son, Dominic, his wife Justine and their three children. "I have had a letter from Tristan and Rosalie. You know I have a rather big birthday coming up—my sixtieth—and while I am not so inclined to count birthdays anymore, Tristan insists it must be celebrated in style. They have invited us all to the coast for a visit and a birthday party. Gabrielle and Féolan too, if they can manage it."

"Oh, they *must* come!" blurted out Madeleine, dropping all pretence of worldliness and jiggling in her seat with excitement along with her brothers. "*Everybody* must come!"

Queen Solange's birthday was after FirstHarvest, Matthieu

remembered. They would spend the best days of summer on the coast and have the biggest party ever. Well, except for Tristan's wedding and his aunt Gabrielle's. The double wedding party had become something of a family legend, but Matthieu had only been six at the time and had fallen asleep before it was over. *This* time, he vowed, he wouldn't miss a single moment.

GABRIELLE WORKED THROUGH that first night until a faint gray light crept through the tiny window of the cabin. Only then, when she was sure that the girls would survive for a few hours without her, did she allow herself to return to the world. She felt blurry and disoriented, as always when she first came away from a long trance. Gazing around the dark room, she could just make out Aline, slumped under a blanket in a nearby chair. Sleep had claimed her, though she had sat awake as long as she could.

It was cold in the cabin. Gabrielle shivered as she stretched out her aching neck and tried to coax some blood into her feet, numb from the long hours of immobility. Then she stood and picked her way to the hearth, where the last embers still glowed red. As quietly as she could, she added wood to the fire and blew on the coals until a small tongue of flame licked up at the fuel. Soon warmth bloomed out into the room. Faintly, she heard the first birdcalls announcing the dawn—it always cheered her, the way birds began their morning songs in the dark, so certain of the coming sunrise. She wondered how Simon was faring, back in Stonewater.

Gabrielle had been nearly six years in La Maronne, living in the Elvish settlement of Stonewater. It had not taken her long to realize that the small Human communities and scattered sheep-ranching

homesteads of the Maronnais highlands had more need for her
healing skills than the Elves. She began visiting the neighboring
villages, traveling as she had sometimes done in Verdeau with her
teacher Marcus, to offer her services. The people had been cautious at first, and shy of the Elvish scouts who traveled with her.
But word soon got out of the marvelously skilled bonemender
who lived among those queer Elf folk but had the Human touch.
These days a steady trickle of Maronnais messengers arrived at
Stonewater requesting her help.

It was the girls' father who had come to her this time. Simon's
rasping cough had preceded him into the healer's lodge. One
look at him—a man in obvious pain, hands swathed in loose
bandages and soot-smeared from head to toe—had galvanized
Gabrielle and Towàs, the young Elvish healer she worked with,
into action. Simon had waved them off—"it's my children I've
come for"—but in the end, Gabrielle had persuaded him to stay
behind with Towàs. A laboring man's hands were his living, and
left untreated they could end up little more than useless scarred
claws. She didn't have to spell out what that would mean to his
family.

Simon had had the sense to let his neighbor Jacques come
along with him. "He wouldn't stay behind, though," said Jacques.
"Couldn't stand watching his girls suffer, and nothing to be done
for them."

Jacques had told her the story as they traveled to the village.
It was an all-too common tale of fire unleashed.

"Must ha' been a spark from the hearth," he said. "You know
it's mostly spruce wood in these parts, and it stays sappy in the
knots. Makes for a crackly fire."

Did they not have a screen, wondered Gabrielle, and then chided herself. People around here made do without many things a princess of Verdeau took for granted. There was no need to assume it was carelessness that put sleeping children by an unscreened hearth.

By the time the family had awakened, the cottage was already lost.

"The parents were sleeping with the baby at the front of the house and were able to get him out safe," said Jacques, "but the flames jumped up between them and the two little girls who slept together beside the fire." Jacques, a burly man whose deep voice rumbled from behind a bush of black beard, raised a big red paw to his face. "When I think of them two…" The booming voice trembled and faded.

Unable to get through the burning half-wall that separated them, the father had grabbed his axe from the wood pile and hacked his way through the outside wall to his shrieking children. "Simon were afraid of hitting 'em with his axe by mistake, but I'm thinking the real danger was that the fire would catch the draft and rush through the opening he made. Course most of the village was there by then, and we had a line of buckets throwing water against the hole, for all the good it did. We all heard the crash when the roof rafter fell."

Simon had pushed his way into the smoke-choked house to find his girls clutched together on the floor, their legs pinned by a fallen burning rafter.

"He hauled that thing off them with his bare hands," Jacques told her, his shaggy head shaking in wonder. "His bare hands."

"Do they live?"

It was Aline, her voice hoarse with sleep but the question sharp and urgent.

"They live." Gabrielle spoke softly; Colette, the grandmother, still snored on her pallet at the back of the house. "They live and are stronger. The burn has begun to heal." She heard Aline's breath sigh out in a long release and gave her this moment to be free of the fear that had hovered over her even in sleep. But it was the truth Aline needed, not false cheer, and so in a while, when the air had softened to gray and she could see the other woman's features, she spoke again. "Aline, it is a long path they must yet travel to be out of danger and longer still to walk and run as before. I will stay as long as I am needed and put all my skill into their healing, but I cannot say how much of the harm that has befallen can be undone."

CHAPTER FIVE

NONE OF THEM WOULD DO. Derkh dropped the last
bracelet into the box where he kept the few articles of
jewellery he had made that were worth saving and closed
the lid. This was work Theo knew nothing of, a skill learned not at
his forge but from the head smith at Stonewater.

All—the necklace, the two bracelets, the delicate knotwork
ring, the ear pendants—were of silver. At first Derkh had worked
in silver because it was the metal favored by the Elves. Later it was
the best he could afford on his modest journeyman's wages. And
silver, he decided, was just wrong for Yolenka.

He had barely laid eyes on her in over a week, thanks to a run
of extra guests at the inn that kept all the staff working over-long
days. Even when he dropped by in the evening, she was too busy
to give him more than a tired smile along with his ale.

That left him plenty of time to think about her. She was
unlike any girl he had ever met—certainly in Greffier, where
the women were quiet and obedient, at least in public. Even in
Verdeau, where people were freer and more outspoken, Yolenka's
forward brashness stood out.

He was no longer intimidated by her manner. He loved it.
It was as if a lifetime of reticence and restraint was set free just
by being with her. He didn't even mind that she had beaten him

to their first kiss, pulling him against the side of the smithy on the very day he had vowed he would kiss her before the sun went down.

He didn't know why she liked him, or if her feelings were as serious as his own. But he realized now in missing her bright presence that he wanted to give her something special.

It should be gold. Derkh had some money set aside—he had been well paid for the hunting set, and although he was still a journeyman bound to give half of what he earned from personal commissions to his master, it was still a handsome sum. Not enough for gold, though.

Bronze? Copper? He shook his head, discouraged now. Yolenka had boasted to him of the artistry of the Tarzine people—the richly patterned textiles with colors like jewels, the elegant crafting of gold and gemstones. He was overstepping himself.

Except…he opened the box again. He had been right to save these pieces. They *were* good. He hadn't mastered the delicacy of Elvish work—no Human ever would—but there was an elusive balance of weight and flow to the design that was distinctive and beautiful.

An idea came to him. He saw the dark burnish of bronze contrasted against Yolenka's warm skin, highlighted with the sheen of gold. He had coin enough for a little gold, enough to brighten the piece and give it richness.

Excited now, his doubts vanished, and Derkh pulled out his quill and ink and began to sketch.

For three days Gabrielle interrupted her care of the girls only to eat and sleep. Colette gave her a hastily stuffed pallet beside her own bed, which she shared in shifts with Aline. As the twins came to consciousness, she soothed their cries and coaxed into them her standard brew of willow bark, comfrey and hawkweed, laced with plenty of honey and a tiny pinch of mandragora—all she dared give them—to ease their hurts and help them sleep. Their wounds were little changed to the eye, but under the surface Gabrielle was steadily pushing back the edges of the damaged tissue. She no longer worried about the girls' survival.

By the fourth day, despite the protective tent she had rigged over their legs and the women's attentive removal of any trapped insects, the honey coating had become grimy.

Bath day, she decided, and wondered how it could be done.

She was just broaching the subject with Aline over a midday meal of barley bread and the salted dried twists of mutton the Maronnais shepherds used as travel fare, when the door opened. Simon stood framed in the light that poured into the cabin, bandages gone, his hands hanging free at his sides.

Aline had not mentioned her husband once in Gabrielle's hearing, and Gabrielle had wondered if there were hard feelings between them. But no—Aline's cry as she sprang to Simon's side was as eloquent as any declaration of love. Gabrielle watched Aline gasp and laugh as she examined Simon's hands, watched his dark eyes well up with tears at the sight of his girls sleeping peacefully.

Later, when Simon sat down to join them at table, Gabrielle asked to see his hands. He flipped them over, spread out his big-knuckled fingers and grinned.

"Can you believe it? And he didn't do hardly anything. Just held onto one of 'em or the other and kind of dozed over it. And then my hand would feel warm and kind of buzzy, like it were a hive of bees, but the burning pain of it would ease off, and I would feel easier in my mind too. And each time, when he was done, the hand looked better."

Towás had done well. Simon's palms were shiny pink, but it was the pink of new skin, not of burned flesh or scarring. They would be sensitive for some time yet, but they would serve him almost as well as before.

"Oh, and before I forget—someone is coming here to see you, m'Lady."

Gabrielle looked up, surprised. Towás, perhaps, coming to help with the twins?

"His name is Féolan. He just rode into town—or whatever that Stonewater place is—as I was getting ready to leave. He says he'll be here by sundown." Simon frowned, struck by a sudden doubt.

"You do know him, m'Lady? He looked something scruffy compared to the others there."

Gabrielle laughed—the first laugh she could remember since arriving at the village—picturing Féolan's response to hearing that a Maronnais shepherd had declared him "scruffy." He would have just returned from trade talks in the Gamier capital of Turleau—a long journey through rough country.

"Oh yes, I know him. He's my husband."

By the time Féolan arrived, the girls had been cleaned up, dosed with medicine, coated (sparingly, this time) with honey and settled back comfortably on their pallets. Simon had taken on the bath project with dispatch, producing two trestle tables, which he set up in an empty livestock shed, and enlisting everyone who could be found in the village to contribute buckets of warm water. He and Aline had carried the girls to the shed and laid them gently on the tables, and Gabrielle had got to work.

Féolan had proved himself equally useful, bringing dinner, a pannier of clean clothes and a tent. After days of sharing a bed and eating hastily prepared peasant fare, an Elvish picnic and a night alone were luxurious gifts.

"How long will you stay?" asked Gabrielle. Colette had been visibly relieved to find she would not need to house and feed Féolan, but only find a patch of ground he could camp on. Still, there was little he could do here.

"I should head back tomorrow." Féolan leaned over the fire to fish out the last packets of *limara*—a rich concoction of dried fruits, nuts, spices and honey, wrapped into a curl of birchbark and soaked before heating in the coals—and gingerly dropped one onto Gabrielle's plate. The evening star had just appeared, shining out over the far hills. "Tilumar is keen to discuss Gamier's trade offer. I just wanted to see you."

Gabrielle couldn't see the sudden brightening of Féolan's eyes in the waning light, but she felt the flare of his desire. Teasing, she carried on their matter-of-fact conversation as though she hadn't noticed, knowing he would sense her own true feelings.

"Can you leave me the tent? I'm sure Aline would rather share her bed with Simon."

"Of course." Féolan smiled wickedly. "If you think you can keep warm without me."

CHAPTER SIX

*T*HE PIRATES SWARMED *through the streets of Chênier, ragged shadows with black-toothed grins and flaming eyes. Madeleine shrank into a doorway as they pounded past her, but the last, a huge mountain of a man, stopped, turned, and the rotten smile broadened into a roar of glee. He grabbed her, brandishing the blade of his great crescent knife and laying it along her throat, and she screamed and screamed but all that came out was...*a hoarse mew that blessedly was enough to wake her.

Madeleine sat up in bed, trying to suppress the wild pounding of her heart. She had overheard talk of pirates that night, not at the dinner table but in the private study where she had hovered in the hallway to listen. Served her right, then, for spying. It was guilt, more than fear, had brought this lurid and overwrought nightmare. So she told herself.

Her nightgown was damp with sweat, cold now in the early spring air. She slipped out of bed and groped in the chest at its foot, finding a new shift by feel in the dark room.

She would never admit it to a soul, but there were times when she missed having a nurse sleep in the room with her. Times like this one, when Rochelle would stir up the fire and chase away the night phantoms with her warm arms and sensible voice.

Since Madeleine's thirteenth birthday so much had changed.

She was a woman now, the crampy bleeding that had come for the first time last month confirming it. She loved the privacy of her room, her new, grown-up dresses and being part of the adult dinners. But she missed—well, she missed Matthieu. A gulf had opened between them, invisible but so hard to cross. Everything he said to her seemed silly or insulting. Everything she said seemed disapproving or superior. He said she was "prissy" and half the time he was right—but she didn't mean to be.

Tonight, though, the gulf had closed up, just for a bit. She saw him again bursting into the dining room with his jacket misbuttoned and his tunic tail poking out in back. When he sat down between Madeleine and Sylvain, only the children had seen the fluffy curl of a gray breast-feather caught in the tousled hair on the back of his head. By unspoken agreement they said nothing, though Sylvain had caught his big sister's eye with a smirk many times through the meal. Finally, at dessert, Madeleine had plucked out the feather with a flourish and planted it in Matthieu's custard where it waved under his breath like a brave little flag. Matthieu, rising to the challenge, had snapped it a smart salute.

Smiling at the memory, Madeleine burrowed into her blankets. She could sleep now. Matthieu had chased away the pirates.

BITING THEIR LIPS with the effort, clutching onto each other's arms for support, Mira and Marie walked slowly but steadily across the road and into Gabrielle's outstretched arms. She felt her eyes well up at the sight, but blinked back the tears and instead gave the girls her most radiant smile. They snuggled against her, and she tugged their neat braids gently. Solemn hazel eyes looked up at her.

"You are such brave wonderful girls, and I am so proud of you."

Shy smiles, just a little wider from Mira. It was easier to tell them apart now, and not only because she knew them better. Mira's gait was draggy in the left leg, the result of a damaged tendon behind the knee. With use it would improve, but Gabrielle thought there would always be a lingering limp.

"You remember what I told you," she added. "You do your stretches four times a day—at every meal and before you sleep. Do them just the way we practiced, and your legs will grow stronger and stronger."

"They'll do their stretches, all right." Simon stood at the doorway to Colette's house, his wife and mother-in-law just behind. "We'll all see to it."

"Then I think that's all." Gabrielle stood and held a hand out to each girl, and together they made their way back to the cabin. She looked now to Aline. "If there's an unexpected setback, you know where to find me. Don't hesitate."

Aline was in tears now, but Simon was more practical. "We can't begin to pay you for what you've done, but whatever we can pay we will."

Gabrielle shook her head. "No, no. There is no fee. Please don't even think of it." She was so thankful she had never had to charge for her services. She couldn't imagine asking these hardworking people, who had already been through so much, for money, or how she could possibly calculate a value for what she did.

"Well, you can't go away empty-handed. Wait here a minute."

Simon disappeared behind the cabin and emerged carrying a bulging burlap sack. It squirmed and gave a muffled squawk.

"Three good chickens in here. If ye'd be so kind to give one to that Towàs fella, by way of my own thanks."

YOLENKA FINGERED, ONCE again, the intricate gold filigree and fine four-strand bronze plait of the necklace. It had taken Derkh a long time to figure out how to incorporate the delicate filigree highlights into the focal point of the necklace—a bold, swooping beaten bronze shape inspired by the deeply flexed wings of an eagle.

"You *made* this?" Amber eyes blazed at him.

Derkh nodded, a little taken aback. Yolenka looked almost angry. Maybe he'd gone too far. "Do you not like it?"

She glared at him. "What is wrong with you? Why you spend your days hammering at horse-metal and buckets, when you have gift like this?" She looked at it again, shaking her head in disbelief. "Is better than anything I ever see here. Better even than much Tarzine work. Style is…beautiful. Different."

Yolenka stood, tossed back her tawny mane and fastened the necklace. The bronze wings spanned from one collarbone to the other, glinting gold and looking just as fabulous against her warm skin as Derkh had hoped. Gods, she took his breath away.

She stalked toward him, raised her face for a kiss that nearly brought him to his knees, and continued her lecture.

"I thank you. I mean this. Is most beautiful thing I have. But you, you are loose in the head. You do work like this, you make and sell everywhere! Nobles, rich men, all will buy! Why you hide here in this piddle town?"

Derkh said nothing as a multitude of answers swirled around in his head. Because he owed Theo, who had apprenticed him, another half-year as a journeyman was the easy answer. Because La Maronne, with its clipped accent and plain-talking country people, felt more like home than the southern town of Chênier might be another. But underlying everything was the fact that he was the son of Greffaire's highest military commander, and "jewelry artisan" was not an occupation that even existed in his mind. It was strange enough to find himself silversmithing as a private hobby.

He was saved a reply by the appearance of his landlady. "Excusing the interruption, Mister Derkh, but you have more visitors." She stressed the word "more" as if his sudden popularity was less than seemly. She frowned. "Very grand and handsome they are too."

A flush of pleasure lit up Derkh's face. There were few enough people likely to arrive as unexpected visitors to his lodgings and fewer still who could be described as "grand."

"A tall man with dark hair, and a woman?" he asked.

The mistress nodded. "The same."

"Bring them—" Derkh glanced around the dark little salon. He felt cramped in here already, with only Yolenka in the room. "No, never mind, we'll come to the door to meet them." He grinned at Yolenka.

"You wanted to meet Elves? Here's your chance."

"I BEAR A special invitation from the Regent of Crow Island and the Blanchette Coast."

Greetings and introductions and small talk had all been

accomplished, and they were now ensconced at a table at Yolenka's inn, where Féolan and Gabrielle happened to be staying. It was Yolenka's first experience as a customer there, and she was rather critical of the service.

"I do better," she had assured them. "You eat here tomorrow, you call for me."

Derkh stared at the elaborate scroll that Féolan had produced with a flourish.

"They want me to come?"

"Tristan made a special point of asking us to deliver the invitation personally, to make certain you come," said Gabrielle. "He says he hasn't seen you in years and you have still never been to the coast."

The DesChênes family would never stop amazing him, Derkh decided. First they had all unhesitatingly befriended a wounded enemy soldier that Gabrielle brought home from the war. Now he was included in a family birthday celebration as though he were a favorite cousin.

It would be a long trip, though. "I don't think Theo will want to let me go for so long," he said doubtfully. The royal seal of Verdeau was impressive, but it held no authority over the citizens of La Maronne.

"I think perhaps he will," said Féolan, producing another scroll. "This is probably the biggest order your master has ever had. You'll be kept busy filling it, I'm afraid, but it comes on condition that the first lot be delivered by you personally and that you stay on at the Queen's pleasure. He'll be well compensated for your time away."

How long had it been since he had traveled with his friends, seen new sights? Derkh was content enough with his new trade and his little town, but now his appetite for adventure awoke. Suddenly he couldn't wait to be on the road.

"We leave in, what, just over a month?" he asked.

Gabrielle and Féolan nodded.

"I'll be ready."

"I too will be ready," Yolenka announced.

Derkh stared at her, not knowing how to reply. Surely she was not inviting herself to the Queen of Verdeau's party?

"What?" she demanded irritably. "You travel south, no? To Chênier, to Blanchette?"

It was Gabrielle who answered. "That's right. Probably we will stay a couple of days in Chênier with my family before traveling on to the coast together."

"I know these places. Big. Busy. Not like this piddle town. I do better there than carry ale and empty piss pots."

Her shoulders rippled in that elaborate eloquent shrug, hands rising to complete the gesture and eyebrows lifting to pull her almond eyes into wide round innocence. "I travel with you, is all I ask. Is all right?"

"You're more than welcome." Gabrielle again, with a warm smile that hid her relief. Derkh didn't feel relieved, not at all. He was thrilled to have Yolenka travel with him. His worry was that she would not come back.

CHAPTER SEVEN

B LANCHETTE WAS A BUSY TRADE PORT and market town, smaller than the royal city of Chênier but more varied and lively. Tristan, when he became regent of the area, took to it immediately, reveling in the noisy docks crowded with trade ships and fishing boats, enjoying the contrast between the rough jumble of lodging-houses, shops, taverns and warehouses dockside and the spacious landscaped manors of the rich merchants and noblemen in the upper town. Beyond them all was the endless Gray Sea, an ever-changing dance of light and wind and water, and on the horizon the just-visible crescent edge of Crow Island.

Almost as soon as his visitors had arrived, Tristan had offered them a tour of the town. Only Justine and Dominic, who knew Blanchette well, and Solange, who was tired from the journey, had turned him down.

"Here's one coming in now." Tristan pointed, leaning far over the railing to get the best view of the ship that had just billowed into sight. A local merchant had been prevailed upon to offer up the balcony that opened out from his second-story office in a warehouse across from the docks, so that the visitors could enjoy a high and private look at the harbor. "When the wind is contrary, they have to row through the straits between the mainland and Crow Island," Tristan said, "but this one is under full sail. You'll get to see them drop the rigging as they approach the harbor."

He hadn't lost his sense of childlike wonder, thought Gabrielle, regent though he was. Tristan was clearly enjoying the sight as much as his son Jerome, who perched on his shoulders. As for Derkh, he was like a questing hound, senses alert, nostrils flared to any new scent. He straightened now, craning his neck.

"Tristan—what are those ships at the far end of the pier?" Half again as big as the coastal traders docked beside them, two great double-masted ships hunkered out in the deepest water. With their sleek lines, thrusting bowsprits and long yardpoles raking back into the sky as though bent in a gale, they stood out from the boxy Basin ships like falcons among pigeons.

"Is Tarzine ships!" Yolenka spoke out. Her proud face filled with eagerness. "I will speak to them. I leave you now." She had clattered down the stairs and emerged into the street below before anyone could stop her.

"Yolenka, be careful!" Derkh shouted down to her. "Those men are—" He was cut off by an impatient wave and a quick grin over her shoulder.

The little group watched Yolenka's progress down the pier. Twice men approached her, only to back off hastily.

"Your friend appears well able to handle Blanchette's seamen," observed Tristan. "I wonder what she said to those poor fellows."

"Probably nothing you'd want your children to hear," Derkh admitted, and Matthieu sniggered.

His sister said nothing, but her eyes never left the small figure stalking toward the foreign ships. She's *formidable*, Madeleine thought, savoring the syllables as they sounded in her head. That's exactly the word. And she wondered what it would be like to face the world with such brash self-confidence.

Féolan was still thinking about the ships. "Are they welcome here, given the raids you told us about?"

Tristan shrugged. "Tarzine traders have always been treated with some suspicion, and they are watched now more carefully than ever. But these men are honest—well, I don't know that they are *honest*, but they are just traders, not pirates. And the very nobles who mutter about their presence here are the ones who clamor for Tarzine rugs and silks. So our merchants are ill-inclined to turn them away."

Yolenka's boasts about her country's artistry had been nothing but the truth. The rug in Gabrielle's chamber in Chênier was of Tarzine make, and by lamp or firelight the colors were so rich they seemed to glow with a life of their own.

"Don't forget the demand for Tarzine jewelry," she said now. "Did you notice the necklace Yolenka is wearing? It's stunning. The filigree work has an almost Elvish look to it, but that bold bronze centerplate is like nothing I've ever seen."

Derkh felt himself flush with pride and pleasure, but everyone was still looking out to sea and it passed unnoticed. Only Féolan's gaze rested on Derkh—but he kept his thoughts to himself.

"MATTHIEU, HURRY UP! You're like an old man falling asleep over his gaming dice." Only he was not asleep, Madeleine knew. He was hunched over the chiggers board like a predatory beast.

Not so long ago, Matthieu had been easy to beat. He was long on impulse and short on patience, going always for the flamboyant

but obvious move. All you had to do to block him was think. But
that had changed. Matthieu had discovered the value of strategy
and learned to slow down long enough to use it. But he had never
taken *this* long at a turn. Madeleine had the uneasy feeling she
had missed something.

Evening had waned into night, and with the younger children
tucked into bed most of the rest of the family had gathered in
what Uncle Tristan called "the sunroom." It wasn't sunny now,
but Madeleine loved the way you could peek up through the big
window set into the roof and see the summer stars. This had been
her favorite room, she remembered, back when she had been little
and lived here instead of in Chênier.

Suddenly Matthieu's taut face relaxed into a triumphant grin.
"I knew it was there somewhere!" He picked up his gray marble
lead dog (for he was the hunter this round, to Madeleine's prey),
o'erhopped three hounds to land on a reverse square, summoned
the two-square falcon token he had pulled earlier and saved, and
landed neatly on the stag. The game was over.

"I missed that completely," admitted Madeleine, chagrinned.
"Nice win, Matthieu." Still she felt rather sulky as she gathered up
the pieces. It was lucky for him she was an adult now and had to
play the part, otherwise she might be tempted to do something
childish and spiteful, as their mother called it.

Matthieu's hand reached out to stop her work. "Play again,
Maddy," he begged.

"I don't really feel like it, Matthieu, it's late and—"

"Exactly," he said. "Mama's been eyeing me across the room,
and only the fact that we're playing nicely together has kept her
from sending me off to bed. As soon as she sees we're done…"

Madeleine was ready for bed herself, but it wasn't often Matthieu got to stay up. Madeleine had not forgotten how it rankled to be excluded from the fun. Not that there's much fun to be had, she thought, eying the adults reading, knitting and chatting around her.

She righted the red stag and moved the fox back to its starting position.

"Quick then, before they notice."

JUSTINE HAD, IN FACT, noticed. She did not miss much when it came to her children. She looked at the two heads bent in conspiracy so close together—one capped with tousled brown hair, the other a startling glory of bright, tumbling curls—and smiled. It was nice to see them getting along for a change, too nice to interrupt.

Of her three children, only Madeleine's coloring took after her grandfather's, King Jerome DesChênes of Verdeau. But in her, it was as if Jerome's rust and wire turned to gold and silk. Madeleine's soft curls were a true strawberry blond—what Jerome had rather poetically called "roses and sunshine."

Madeleine straightened up, and in the lamplight her features looked older, more defined. Justine caught a sudden glimpse of her daughter at fifteen or sixteen—a young beauty with round sky-blue eyes and hair every young man who gazed upon her would wish to touch. I should lock her up right now, she thought and gave a false little titter as if to convince herself she was only joking.

DOMINIC HAD JUST raised an inquiring eyebrow at his wife when the door was opened by one of Tristan's men.

"Excuse me, sire. There is a messenger from Maquard. Urgent."

"Bring him in, man!" Tristan, who had been to all appearances asleep and snoring on Rosalie's lap, was wide-awake and on his feet. He strode across the room to meet the messenger as he entered.

"A Tarzine ship was spotted yesterday by a fisherman, sire. We've been watching her, and she's put in just around the point from Maquard Bay, secret-like. I left before anything more happened, but everything points to a raid. They'll have the dinghies in the water by now, I warrant."

"Good. I hope they do!" said Tristan with grim satisfaction. "Look how bold they have grown, Dominic, attacking within spitting distance of Blanchette itself."

Ten years ago, Maquard had been a tiny fishing village nestled just east of Blanchette. But as warehouse space in Blanchette became more crowded and more dear, merchants trading from and with Gamier looked to nearby Maquard for cheaper storage space. Maquard's harbor was neither as deep nor as large as Blanchette's, but it was adequate for the smaller traders, and in recent years Maquard had grown into a small market town in its own right. It would be a rich target for pirates.

"This is our chance to see our lads in action," announced Tristan. "The message has gone to the garrison?" he asked in the same breath.

The messenger nodded. "As you commanded." Tristan had installed garrisons at key points along the Verdeau coast and had provided two fast well-trained horses to designated messengers at every significant coastal settlement.

"Good. Let's see then, how these Tarzines manage against soldiers instead of farmers and fishermen." He looked at Dominic.

"You coming?"

His brother grinned. "Wouldn't miss it."

As if struck simultaneously by the same thought, the two men turned to their alarmed wives.

"Tristan, you don't have to go!" said Rosalie. Her arms circled her swelling belly. "That's what the soldiers are for. You have children who depend on you now."

"So do they, Rosie girl. So do they." The childish excitement gone, Tristan was quietly sober now. He knelt in front of Rosalie and rested his hands over hers. "You know how I feel about leaders who hide behind their men. I'll be careful, that I promise you—but I intend to see these pirates well and truly routed tonight."

Féolan cleared his throat. Gabrielle, taken up in the drama unfolding before her, had all but forgotten him. Now, she realized, she had one more to worry about. He smiled apologetically.

"I think I'd better go to keep an eye on your brother," he said. "You know he has a tendency to get carried away."

The room was suddenly filled with purpose. "Then let's get ready," said Tristan simply. "We ride back with this man, here, as soon as may be. Meet in front of the stables."

He turned to his guard. "See that our horses are prepared and that this fellow has a fresh one. We'll ride with the garrison if we're in time, or follow if we're not."

The room emptied, leaving Madeleine and Matthieu forgotten at the games table.

THEY STARED AT each other over the chiggers board. Madeleine watched Matthieu's expression change from blank shock to urgency, as though a fire had been kindled under his skin.

"Let's go."

"Go? Where?" asked Madeleine. He couldn't mean bed, not with his eyes lit up like a First-Month fire.

"To see the battle! Maddy, it's only to Maquard, just down the road. It's perfect!"

"Don't be daft. They'd never let you."

"Maddy, listen." Matthieu was in an agony of impatience. "We'll just wait till they're gone, take our horses and follow them. They'll never know we're there."

Madeleine was shaking her head before he was halfway done.

"Matthieu, stop right now. No. The answer is no. This isn't players fooling at fighting—it's real. It's dangerous. We'd be in the way and—oh, I'm not even going to argue it. It's just ridiculous."

Matthieu's face darkened and his jaw jutted out. She hadn't dissuaded him; she had goaded him on.

"You're afraid," he said. "You're afraid of everything now! You won't even risk getting your gown dirty. But I'm going, with or without you. I won't get in the way—I'm just going to find a safe place away from the battle and watch my dad and Tristan kick those pirates into the ocean. *You* can stay home and be a little lady and never have an adventure ever again, for all I care."

He jumped up from the table, scattering the chiggers pieces, and leaned his face close to her. "And if you rat on me, Maddy, I swear by the dark gods—I will never trust you or be your friend again!" And with that he headed for the door.

Madeleine watched him go, trying to pull The Right Thing

to Do from the confused tangle of thoughts in her head. She couldn't let Matthieu go riding off into the night alone; that was clear. He probably wouldn't even remember the way. She would have to tell Justine and stop him.

And never have an adventure again. The words hit her like a slap. It was the little fear that whispered to her sometimes at night—that under the pretty clothes and elegant dinners, adult life was essentially dull. And in spite of herself, she imagined the thrill of what Matthieu had proposed—the two of them, riding down a dark road together, witnessing the triumphant defense of the Verdeau Coast.

"Matthieu, wait," she said.

CHAPTER EIGHT

D RESSED IN HIS CUSTOMARY BLACK, Turga had little fear of being spotted as he eased himself out of the fighting and began to climb the hill overlooking the beach. Only the gold gleaming at his neck and wrist might betray him in the moonlight. He had affected his dark attire, so at odds with the taste of most of his countrymen, to stand out from the common rank and file and proclaim his authority. Tonight, though, he was content to blend in.

The slope was sandy, crumbling under his boots, and he was compelled to sheath his sword and grasp with both hands at the tough clumps of sedge and dune-vetch to pull himself up.

The climb was hardly worth the bother. Turga had hoped that from a high vantage he would have a better sense of the momentum of battle. But although the moon lit up the open ocean like a beacon, it only glanced at the riotous struggle beyond the hill in stingy fitful glimpses. Impossible to say who had the upper hand.

He had, perhaps, grown a little too bold, venturing so close to Blanchette. Still, it had been a free ride up to now and only a matter of time before even these soft Krylians mounted some kind of defense. A spirited defense, he had to admit, both swifter and more ferocious than he could have predicted.

Well, it was good for his men to face trained warriors for a change—kept them sharp. He would let them fight a while longer, and then move them back to the ship before too many were lost. When victory was in doubt, it was always better to retreat in strength. In a rout, they would be slaughtered trying to launch the dinghies.

He allowed his eyes to roam over the battle one last time before turning to make his way down. He did not intend to be cut off from his own ship. In fact, he would walk along the ridge of hill a little farther, descend well away from the melee and sound the retreat from the water's edge.

A rustle, nearly at his left hand, brought him to a halt. Keen eyes narrowed to slits swept the dark landscape before resting on the large clump of shrubbery before him. One tawny hand slid to his sword-hilt while the other drifted out to finger a thorny spray of foliage.

Doubtless it was just some night creature, made restless by his presence. But Turga had not become warlord of land and sea by turning his back on potential enemies. He pulled his sword and thrust aside an armful of prickly branches.

IT WAS HER dream all over again. As Matthieu shrank back against her, Madeleine stared, frozen, at the pirate towering over her. Backlit by the moon, he was a dark silhouette—all but the flash of teeth as he grinned at the two children huddled behind the furze bush.

But his teeth aren't rotten, she thought, her mind looping into nonsense. His teeth aren't rotten, so this can't be a dream!

Matthieu gave a sudden heave and was on his feet, groping at his side for his hunting knife. "C'mon, Madeleine, he's not that big!" he shouted. "We can—"

The man was not so big, perhaps, but he had the speed and power of a mountain cat. Matthieu was disarmed, pinned against the pirate's side and a hair away from disembowelment before Madeleine was fully standing.

"Leave him alone!" She shrieked at the man in fear and rage, but at the sharp gesture of his sword she fell silent. He nodded approvingly, stepped back a pace and stared at her. The white teeth flashed again, and he spoke now, a deep bass voice pitched quiet and calm, the words a blur of meaningless sound.

The gestures were clear enough. He backed Matthieu up against his sister at sword point, rummaged in his coat and produced a length of rope. The smell of tar rose to Madeleine's nostrils as rough sticky fibers bit into her wrist. He trussed their hands together, Matthieu's behind his back, Madeleine's in front, and Madeleine understood that any struggle on her part would wrench cruelly at her brother's arm sockets. Then the pirate's fingers closed like a smith's vice around Madeleine's upper arm. A gleaming sword tip came to rest, first under her chin and then under Matthieu's. They didn't need to understand the man's muttered words to understand the threat.

And then they were dragged off, across the ridge of the hill and down toward the beach. They had to scurry crablike to make it down the hill with their hands joined, and the pirate gave them no time to place their feet but simply hauled them along, yanking them upright when they stumbled, the hard fingers biting into Madeleine's arm if she faltered.

He hustled them through the soft sandy soil at the foot of the hill toward the sea, and for a while Madeleine was in such shock she could not think ahead to their destination. But when her feet hit the hard-packed ridges of sand that marked the high-tide line, her head snapped up and she saw the great hulk of ship looming against the silvery sky.

A cry of fear escaped her, and she dug in her heels and heaved back against the hard grip of the man's hand. If they were taken on that ship, there would be no going back.

But resistance was futile, even had he not been so strong. The sword swept up against Matthieu's neck and pressed until Matthieu was forced back against her. The pirate pressed his face into Madeleine's ear and spoke to her with quiet menace. No bluster, only cold threat, and she knew beyond certainty that if she cried out again Matthieu would be dead.

Minutes later they came upon the dinghies studded on the wet sand.

THE TARZINES WERE no cowards, despite their preference for help-less prey. They fought with a fierce gusto bordering on glee, and they moved faster than any humans Féolan had encountered. Still, the garrison at Blanchette was large and well trained, and he had little doubt the pirates would soon be driven back.

He was never sure what made him glance down the beach. The air was full of shouting and screams, groans and roared curses. Even his Elf-ears could not have picked out one young voice. Yet something carried enough to prick at him—perhaps just the hint of a sound in the wrong register for fighting men. Perhaps a drifting wisp of the children's fear.

Precious seconds ticked by as Féolan fought his way clear of the worst press of battle. But once he gained the sidelines, the night swallowed him. Slipping behind a twisted little pine tree, he scanned the beach, his vague sense of "wrongness" swelling suddenly to sharp alarm.

There was a figure among the dinghies, he saw. Even in the dark, his sharp eyes noted the strange, hunched shape, the clumsy way it moved. A man with a large burden, perhaps, or...

The moon sailed free of the shredded clouds and, as though drawn to its own likeness, flooded down onto Madeleine's hair, turning her golden curls into a gleaming beacon. She sat with Matthieu in a dinghy, her round, frightened face a pale moon on earth.

Féolan was running before his mind had taken in what he had seen. Someone, somehow, had Dominic's children.

A dark figured heaved the dinghy into the water, hopping over the gunnel as he pushed off. The Elf's long legs flew over the sandy ground. Even if the pirate made ship, he would be aboard without a crew. Féolan could have the children safely away while the battle ashore yet raged. He would swim to the god-blighted ship and haul himself up the anchor rope if need be.

MATTHIEU'S ARMS HURT so badly the pain almost blotted out his fright. Being hauled down the hill and across the beach had been worst for him, with his arms bound behind him. Every misstep and stumble had yanked his shoulders backward from their sockets. Clambering into the little boat had been worse. Now, relieved at least to be sitting down, he pulled his left leg over the seat to straddle it sideways and take the strain off his shoulders. He wished he could look at Maddy. He wondered if she was crying. His own face was a mess of dribbling tears and snot—and no way to wipe it.

Now the tears threatened again and along with them a liquid shaft of fear that made his legs watery and weak. The shore was receding fast, lurching away over the shoulder of the pirate in creaking oar-thrusts, and the thought that it might be his last sight of home brought a great choking sob out of his throat. He felt Madeleine squirm closer behind him, her cold hands groping for and then closing over his. Matthieu stared at the beach as though he could hold it still in his gaze. In that moment he saw it: a tall slight figure, indistinct against the dark shore but racing like the very wind, racing so fast it took only moments to realize who it was.

"Féolan," Matthieu breathed. He snapped his face away, afraid to look in case the pirate noticed his flare of hope. They would be rescued. He would go home…

GODS OF THE DEEP, he would have to swim after all. If he was seen giving chase in a dinghy, all the pirate had to do was hold the children's lives hostage. He could neither risk a bow shot nor continue the pursuit. Secrecy was his only ally here.

Stripping off his tall boots and his coat, Féolan plunged silently into the sea. "Grant me stealth and secrecy now," he prayed, wishing he could black his face. He did not follow directly after the dinghy, but set out for the ship's stern, hoping to angle away from the man's line of vision.

He was twenty feet out, no more, when he heard the whistle shrilling through the night air. The pirate was standing in the dinghy, facing the shore where his men still fought. He blew three, long piercing blasts, half-deafening to Féolan from where he treaded water, and then a long series of staccato trills. Carried and amplified by the water, the whistle had an instant effect on the Tarzine men.

Casting stealth aside, Féolan put his head down and swam with everything he had.

CHAPTER NINE

T HE WHISTLE SHRILLED THROUGH the dark air. A retreat? Dominic fervently hoped so—it was about time these poxy thugs were served their own poison. He wrenched his sword, locked against a young pirate's blade, in an abrupt half-circle to free it, drew back for the lunge—and gaped in astonishment. His opponent had sprung backward a good three paces and taken to his heels. All around him, Tarzine men were sprinting for the water.

It was not a retreat to Dominic's mind, so much as a headlong rout. Basin soldiers were drilled in the importance of an orderly retreat, with a rearguard keeping the opposing forces at bay. To allow an entire army to rush pell-mell from the field was to invite devastating losses.

The Tarzines were not, however, an entire army but a compact strike force, and Dominic soon saw the logic of their sudden flight. Yes, a few men fell to a hastily thrown spear or lucky sword-thrust in the back, but most gained the beach well ahead of the pursuing soldiers. They had to, or they would have no time to launch their boats. These had obviously been pre-assigned; without breaking stride, four or five men grabbed onto each boat and with one great heave had it afloat. With a man on each of the four oars, the little dinghies flew over the water.

Some of Tristan's men lunged into the sea after them, but the horns soon called them back. They were ill-equipped to fight in chest-high water. Besides, their job here was defense—not slaughter.

FÉOLAN GLANCED OVER his shoulder. The boats would soon be upon him. The crews' attention, though, was fixed shoreward. With luck, he might still remain undetected and broach the ship. What more he might do, on a vessel swarming with enemies, he did not try to guess.

He was tiring too. The ocean was colder and choppier than the lakes he was used to, and his breath was already short from battle and his long sprint. As the first boat to pass close by him drew near, he pulled air deep into his lungs and sank into the black water.

He managed to stay under the surface until that dinghy passed and to rise unnoticed. Time only to suck in a few gasps of air until two more boats overtook him. This time, his chest burned with the need to breathe as he counted ten slow oar strokes. A few sweet breaths, barely time for the gasping to settle into a less urgent rhythm, and he was down in the cold arms of the ocean again.

But his luck failed. Though he escaped detection, the inky underwater darkness blinded him. He did not see the oars cutting through the water, did not know that on a call from the bow lookout one boat veered sharply to correct its course.

As Féolan floated unseen in the dark, an oar blade, pulled with all the brawn and will of a fleeing seaman, struck the back of his head. The world dissolved into a tumbled black void, without up or down or any other clear direction. Without land. Without air. He floundered for the surface—and found nothing.

Eight dinghies clustered around the great ship. Chains rattled and creaked as the boats were hauled, four to a side, onto the deck. A whistle shrilled, and with a great flapping tumult the huge triangular sails were unfurled, raked back on an angle like a stooping falcon. From the long thrusting bowsprit a last sail grew up to the night sky—then, like a dream that fleets through sleep and is lost, the ship was gone.

TRISTAN PACED THE water's edge, restless with the jangly energy that always remained with him after a battle. The small bundle he happened upon barely caught his interest—just some pirate castoffs, lost in the retreat. He prodded at it with his foot, spreading open the soggy cloth to reveal tall leather boots, supple and soft-soled.

"Dark gods, take me." What were Féolan's boots doing here? Tristan looked wildly around, hoping to catch sight of his brother-in-law. He hadn't seen him since...His heart sank. He couldn't remember seeing Féolan since midway through the battle.

Sharp with worry, he collared the nearest handful of men and sent them searching. But his mind nagged at him. Boots, stashed at the water's edge...They could not, as he first feared, have been left by pirates who stole them from Féolan's body. The Tarzines had had no time, in that breakneck retreat, for looting. No, Féolan had done this himself, and that meant...

Tristan set off again along the surf line, jogging now, his eyes scanning the dark waves. Once again the moon, beloved of Elven folk, was kind. Its silvered rays danced over a dark shape bobbing gently in the tide swell.

Dominic found his brother in time to see him struggling back to shore, his arms clasped around a limp body.

"Who is it, Tristan?"

"It's Féolan."

Together they dragged Féolan out of the water and laid him gently in the sand. Fear tightened Tristan's voice.

"Dom, I think he's drowned."

IT WAS A RECENT recruit to the Blanchette garrison, the son of a fisherman, who pressed the water from Féolan's lungs and brought him, coughing and retching, back to them. The young man stepped back, overawed by his brush with royalty.

"He should be all right now, sire...sires." The poor fellow blushed and bobbed his head, and Tristan pulled his attention away from his friend long enough to rescue him. He got to his feet and clapped the soldier on his shoulder.

"My most hearty thanks to you. What is your name, my man?"

"Barnaby, sir. Sire."

"Barnaby, I will see that the garrison commander knows of your quick action. You have saved my friend's life. But you'd best report back to your unit now."

"Yes, sire. I will." And the shy fellow escaped at the speed of a retreating Tarzine pirate.

By the time Tristan turned back to his friend, Féolan was breathing more comfortably, and Dominic was fingering the back of his head.

"Tris, he's been wounded. See if you can get a torch over here—it's too dark to see."

Féolan's hand waved off the suggestion. "Never mind that." His voice was surprisingly strong. He planted a hand in the sand, pushed himself to sitting and turned to Dominic. "It's your children. They've been taken. I tried to save them, but I was too late. From the depths of my heart, I am sorry."

CHAPTER TEN

HOW LONG HAD THEY BEEN SHUT UP in here? Madeleine squirmed on the thick coils of rope, trying to find space and air where there was none. The blackness smothered her, and the conviction grew that they would die here, shut up in a box, their nostrils filled with the reek of hemp and tar and rancid fish oil. Panic, kept at bay by a thin thread of will these long hours, swelled within her.

Turga had hustled them into the great storage crate as soon as they set foot on his ship. It was fixed to the deck, stocked with extra ropes and other supplies. Turga and a crew member had hoisted them over the side, pushed them down and lowered the lid. The sound of the lock clicking into place had frightened Madeleine more than anything that had happened so far.

At least their hands were now free, and the children had clutched at each other while they listened to the purposeful chaos that followed: the creak of chains and thud of dinghies being hoisted aboard, shouts and orders, whistle blasts and the sudden crackle and snap of sails. The gentle rocking of the anchored ship changed to a sensation Madeleine remembered from childhood trips to Crow Island—the breast and fall of a ship on open water.

"They got away," she said. She had been waiting, she now realized, for a rescue, clinging to the belief that, however bad it seemed, things would turn out right in the end. Now the bleak truth sank its evil claws into her heart. Some nightmares you don't wake up from.

"They'll come after us," said Matthieu. "Don't worry, Maddy. Dad will save us."

"He doesn't even know where we are!" Madeleine's voice was shrill with fear and accusation. She clamped down on her lips before more spilled out: Why did you have to come here? Why couldn't you listen?

"Maddy, I'm sorry." Matthieu's voice was a trembly whisper. "It's all my fault this happened." A sniff, and another, and then Madeleine felt Matthieu wiggle around and drag an arm across his face. "I was so stupid."

Somehow, Matthieu's penitence allowed Madeleine to be generous. She squeezed her brother's hand. "You *were* stupid, but so was I. I could have stopped you, and I didn't. We both decided to come. So now, at least we're here together."

They were brave words, and they felt even braver when Matthieu told his sister that he was sure Féolan had spotted them. But then time crawled on, and the black closeness pressed down, and despair whispered to her. Nobody knew where they were going. Nobody even knew where the Tarzine lands were. Nobody knew who it was who had captured them. There would be no escape.

But she would not, could not, die in this hideous cage. She couldn't breathe; she couldn't move. The dark had taken on weight and texture and it would press the life right out of her.

The first breathy sound that escaped her snapped her self-control. She screamed, and then she couldn't stop. She was shrieking, kicking, beating at the box.

"Maddy, stop!" Matthieu tried in vain to pull down her hands. "Stop, you're scaring me!" He was yelling now too, the fear a contagion.

Flooding light blinded them and silenced their cries. Madeleine blinked and squinted, grasping after her wits as the crate's lid was opened wide. Strong arms hauled them onto the deck. The children stood dazed, awed by the sight that surrounded them.

The endless silver ocean stretched out to the horizon, lit up by a breathtaking red dawn that spread its glory over the world with no care for human struggles.

Madeleine had a confused view of a crowded but tidy deck and men in once-bright clothes, now faded from salt and sun, busy at their tasks. All busy but one, sitting cross-legged with an expanse of ochre sailcloth spread over his lap, who put down his needle and stared at her in hungry appraisal. She looked away quickly, but not before she saw the sly grin spread across his narrow face.

The two men who had freed them barely glanced their way. They grasped hold of the children and hustled them down a narrow ladder. It was dark below decks, lit only by the two shafts of light that pierced down from the fore and aft hatches. Shadowy rows of hammocks strung two deep, holds stacked with crates and barrels fastened down with rope, a roughed-in stall crowded with bleating animals—all these passed by as the children were marched the length of the hull toward the narrow forward hold.

There they stopped in front of a solid wood wall spanning the breadth of the ship, broken by a barred iron door. Their captors pulled back the bolts and pushed them inside. Madeleine listened to the dry grating of the bolts being shoved home. This was her life now, she supposed: the sound of locks.

She looked around the dim, almost triangular space. There was just enough floor space to walk a few paces, and a raised platform fitted into the tapering bow. It stank—she smelled urine, and that fishy smell that seemed to permeate the wood of the ship...and body odor.

Matthieu nudged her and pointed. Huddled into the narrow end of the platform, draped in a ratty blanket that made him almost invisible against the dark planking, sat a boy. He regarded them silently for a moment and then scooted to the edge of the bed—it served, it seemed, as a bed—and stood.

He was taller than Madeleine, a little older too, she judged. Rough-cut straw hair, rough-woven clothing with patched knees—a peasant boy. He, in his turn, was taking in the children's fine cloaks and garments. He hesitated, cleared his throat and spoke.

"I guess we're all equal here, whatever we are back home. I am Lucien." His formality dissolved into a sad fleeting smile. "People just call me Luc."

DOMINIC COULD NOT stop moving. Dawn was not far off, and still they had no workable plan. He needed to go after his children—*now*—and with every passing hour they drew farther away.

Dominic and the others had wakened the whole household on their return: just telling what had happened and everyone's shocked reactions had taken up precious time. It had been terrible to watch the blood drain from Justine's face, to see the soft edges of sleep transform into terror. That terror gripped her still, Dominic knew, though she had pushed it back enough to sit at the big table with the others, searching for some plan that would bring back her babies.

Derkh was not with them. His eyes had grown big on hearing the news, and then he had blurted out, "I'll be back," and bolted from the room. They had seen no sign of him since. Well, it wasn't Derkh's family or his problem. Dominic put the man from his mind.

"All right, let's go over it again." Tristan, sensing Dominic's growing agitation, took the reins. "We have to go after them, that much is obvious. But there are two huge obstacles. The first, I would take my chances with: Our ships are designed for coastal waters, not the open sea, and our sailors aren't used to sailing more than a day or two away from landmarks. But the second has to be solved: We don't know where the pirate ship is headed."

"We need someone who can guide us to the Tarzine lands," Gabrielle said. "Can we pay one of the Tarzine navigators now in port?"

"I think Derkh is trying to find out just that," put in Féolan quietly. He sat with a wad of cold toweling pressed to the back of his head. He was pale, taxed by the pounding pain that radiated through his skull, but Gabrielle had said there would be no lasting damage.

Tristan smacked himself on the forehead. "Gods, I am stupid! Of course, he has gone to find Yolenka!"

Dominic stopped his pacing. Yolenka had even less reason than Derkh to help them. Yet here was a thread of hope. If her heart was as expansive as the rest of her nature, surely she would at least translate for them and plead their case…

It was a long wait, long enough that Dominic was ready to ride down to the docks himself to speak with any Tarzine who had a bit of Krylian. Only Solange was able to persuade him to eat breakfast first, with her usual practical sense: "You will not help your children by refusing food, Dominic. You must eat while you can."

He had just forced in the first bite of bread when Derkh returned with Yolenka in tow.

She surveyed them with fierce amber eyes.

"So, we chase Turga. Take back your childrens. Is past time somebody stops this man."

Justine beat Dominic to a reply. She stood, took Yolenka's hands and asked, "You will help us do this, Yolenka?"

"I help already. You sail in good Tarzine ship, fast, with full crew. They do not fight Turga for you, only sail—is agreed?"

Dominic barked out a laugh that was dangerously close to a sob. Justine was already in tears, her arms tight around Yolenka's neck.

"Yes, agreed! Absolutely agreed!"

"Good." Yolenka pried open Justine's hands and pulled them gently away. "Will cost you much money. Is risk for them, to go against warlord. You will pay?"

"Whatever it takes," assured Dominic.

"Definitely," agreed Tristan. "But just for interest—what will it take?"

The sum brought a momentary impressed silence to the room. Solange ended it.

"Consider it done," she said.

LUC WAS FROM a Gamier fishing port north of Batinie. He had been captured when the pirates raided his town, some days ago. He didn't know if his family had survived.

"They took one other besides me," he told them. "Just a little guy, he was, still with his milk teeth. He was scared to climb the rope ladder up to the ship—he cried so hard when they made him go up. And then didn't he slip and fall?" Luc fell silent and took to scratching at his wrists with fingers red and rough from outdoor work.

"Bedbugs," he said shortly, noting their silent stares. He held out his wrist, dotted with raised red bumps. "Must be in the blanket they gave me." He scratched again, thoroughly, intently, as though it were an important chore.

"What happened to the little boy?" asked Matthieu.

Luc said nothing at first. He stared woodenly past the iron door, and his eyes grew red with suppressed tears, and Madeleine understood he was reliving that moment. Finally he shrugged in baffled anger.

"They let him drown. They just sailed off and left him in the water."

It seemed they would never get underway. Dominic forced himself to clamp down on his impatience and think. Without a viable plan, they might as well be chasing after shadows.

"What guarantee do we have that these men are honest?" he asked Yolenka. "What is to keep them from selling us out to this…"

"To Turga," she finished. "Is no guarantee." Her level gaze challenged him. "You think is better, go in one of your little washtub boats."

"Dominic, it's our best chance." Tristan's hand, steadying on his shoulder.

"This captain, he lost ship and two fingers to Turga," said Yolenka. "Maybe is not honest—but he has no love for pirates. He say you kill Turga is good, save him more trouble."

"This isn't about killing Turga!" protested Dominic. "It's about saving my children."

"Sure." Yolenka's shoulders rippled and flexed in an elaborate shrug. "But captain can believe what he likes."

Her golden eyes flashed as she took charge of the little gathering and laid out her plan. "You cannot go in with army big enough to overpower a warlord on his own ground. Is no possible. Must have small group, secret in purpose.

"I go," she announced, "to speak for you. As guide. I am traveling dancer." Yolenka raised her arms above her head and began a languid sinuous shimmy that left every man in the room gaping. She caught their expressions and sneered.

"Is whore dancing," she said dismissively. "Takes no skill. They like this in badlands."

"I bet they do," breathed Tristan, earning himself a swift elbow in the ribs from Rosalie.

"So," said Yolenka, "who else comes?"

Dominic stepped in front of Tristan, cutting off his brother's eager step forward.

"I do."

"You are father, is certain you go. Who else?"

Not Justine or Tristan, it turned out, though both wished to. Tristan was reined in sharply by his mother: "You are the Regent of Crow Island and the Blanchette Coast, which is currently subject to frequent pirate attack. Your duty lies here with the defense of the coast." Justine was dissuaded more gently, by the specter of a mishap that might leave little Sylvain orphaned.

Derkh, announcing, "You aren't going over there without me," was met by a brilliant flash of teeth.

"You know to make weapons?" asked Yolenka.

"Of course."

"Is perfect. You sell weapons and jewelwork—get rich from Turga himself!"

Dominic looked up quizzically. That was a bit much, asking a blacksmith to masquerade as a jewelry craftsman. How would they maintain that charade?

Yolenka caught his look. "What?" Her gaze bored into him, sharp as a bird of prey.

"Yolenka." Derkh laid a hand on her arm, smoothing ruffled feathers. "Dominic doesn't know I make jewelry, that's all. I haven't really told anyone."

Now the sharp gaze swiveled over to Derkh, the eyebrows raised in disbelief. "You hide this in cellar, why? Is gift you have!" She fingered her necklace, lifting the bronze and gold centerplate so it caught the light. "He make this. I sell twenty of these in one day in Tarzine market, easy. Lucky I tell him bring his pieces to sell in Blanchette."

They had no time to wonder at this revelation. Gabrielle asked to go in case the children were hurt and was welcomed into the little band as a seller of remedies and stitcher of wounds.

"Charms, too, is very good," suggested Yolenka.

Féolan was accepted as a musician, though he would have to work with Yolenka on ship to learn a suitable accompaniment to her dance style.

The problem of Dominic's disguise stumped them. He was soon to be king of Verdeau and had never before felt inadequate to any task, but now he seemed the only one in the room who could not boast of some special talent.

"Is no matter," assured Yolenka. "We think on ship."

She surveyed their little band. "Five. Is good number, not too big. Is anyone else must come?" she asked Dominic.

He considered, shook his head. "I don't think so."

"We add just one more then," she announced. "Fighter. Bodyguard. Women go into badlands, they need strong protection—especially whore dancers. And we need good fighter, maybe, to help steal back children."

Derkh's pale face flushed. "You have us—that's what we are going for, to fight!"

Yolenka's look, fond but dismissive, did nothing to bring down his color. "You are strong and brave, yes. But we need fighter with training, man who can meet Turga's best."

It was Tristan who spoke up. "Yolenka, if you think we need more men, I can assign as many as you like. But if you are looking for better fighters, you won't find them—not in Verdeau. Derkh was personally trained by the commander of his country's military, and Féolan is faster with blade and bow than anyone I ever saw. Each of these men has saved my life. Together with my brother, there is no one I would trust more in a battle."

Yolenka swept her eyes over them, reappraising, lingering over Derkh. At last she nodded.

"Then, no. Smaller is better, I think. Unless you want more?" She turned to Dominic, acknowledging, if grudgingly, that this was really his venture.

He shook his head slowly. "No, not knowing the country, I will trust to your judgment. And you are right: a smaller group can travel with less notice.

"Which brings me to the next problem. How on earth will we know where he has taken them?"

"I know where he takes them." Yolenka's voice was flat, her face grim and still. The amber eyes when they met Dominic's had lost their fierce pride. He read pity there, and old pain, and felt a bolt of fear for his babies.

"He takes them to Baskir," Yolenka announced. "To slave auction."

CHAPTER ELEVEN

"WHEN ALL ARE HOME SAFE, we will celebrate something better than an old woman's birthday."

When, not *if.* The quiet courage and optimism of the word was exactly what Dominic had learned to expect from his mother. Solange would never admit the specter of failure, not while she had the least scrap of hope. Certainly not at this dockside farewell.

She does look old, thought Dominic. Had a bad night, despite the brave face. Solange's features were drawn and sallow, the age lines harsher in the morning light than was usual.

Well, they were all of them getting older. Justine liked to tease Dominic about the grizzle at his temples and beard, but to be honest he hardly noticed the changes in her. Only when Gabrielle came to visit—Gabrielle, who looked as fresh and willowy as she had at twenty—did he really see the march of time through his family. How strange it must be for her, he thought, to watch us wither.

Dominic gave himself a mental shake. He was a practical man, no philosopher, and he was not withered yet. It was time to set sail.

Gabrielle was already making her good-byes with the women. Dom turned first to Tristan.

"It's killing me not to come with you—you know that, right?" Tristan's hard grip on Dominic's forearm underlined his words. "Just say the word, and I'm on board."

Dominic hesitated. There was nothing he would like better than to have his brother at his side. But more than defending the coast was at stake. Dominic knew that Solange was thinking about the kingship too, when she insisted Tristan remain behind. She would not talk about bad outcomes, but she would plan for them nonetheless, because she was queen. If they were killed in this attempt—and they might well be—then Verdeau would still have a worthy heir to the throne.

Dominic shook his head. "This one's mine, Tris. But I'll miss you, brother."

Then it was Justine. After fifteen years together, few words were needed.

"Bring them home, Dom," she whispered as he held her close.

"I will," he promised. High spirits help him, he was sailing blind into an unknown land with a dancing girl as his guide, but he held his promise as an oath. He would return with his children—or not at all.

NIGHT WAS COMING on again. Madeleine's throat tightened into a hard knot at the thought. Evil as their days were, it was the nights that she feared. When the blackness closed down upon them, the crawling endless hours eating at their courage, the hope in her heart shredded away like mist.

Was this their sixth night? It didn't seem to matter anymore. They had been at sea long enough that Madeleine could find grim amusement at how horrified she had been at the rusty bucket in the corner of their cell, which served as a communal toilet. She had not thought she would ever be able to relieve herself in full view of a strange boy—not until the cramping took her and her bowels, loosened by fear and the brackish water that was their only drink, decided the matter for her. The three children had all filled the hold with the reek of their waste, sharing the shame of it as they shared the itch of bed lice and the wretched food that two days' hunger had taught her to eat.

By day they talked, they helped each other, they argued. Each kept up a brave front for the others. They learned to make the long hours pass with Matthieu's riddles or Madeleine's retelling of their favorite childhood stories—even lessons from Luc on the parts of a ship and fishing methods. They learned too, to avoid talk of home, the memories that sapped their strength and left them in helpless tears. At night, though, Madeleine was alone. They were each alone. She felt Matthieu's back pressed against hers, and held him when he cried in the dark, but she couldn't beat back the black shadow that enclosed him. She heard Luc sometimes too, snuffling and gasping, trying to hide his weeping.

The ship lurched—an alarming sideways yaw that was replicated exactly by Madeleine's stomach. Matthieu groaned, his arms pressed tight around his waist. The seas had been growing rougher all day and now, it seemed, the night would bring worse. Another high-cresting climb and lurching sideslip followed the first. They landed hard, the impact jostling the three children against each other on the platform that served as bed, chair and table.

"Breathe slow and deep," offered Luc. "Go with the roll; don't fight it."

Madeleine didn't have much hope it would work. Before long, she thought, we'll be adding the stink of vomit to this pit.

The ship screeched in protest as another wave hit, the usual creak and groan of timbers giving way to an almost human shriek.

"What was that?" yelled Matthieu. His eyes, round and wild, strained into the dim half-light. "Are we breaking up?"

"No, be easy," said Luc. "A big ship like this ain't worried about a hard swell—she's just complainin'. Even our fishing boats could handle this. It's nasty if you're not used to it, but there's no danger."

No danger. A funny choice of words.

Only today, Madeleine had learned just what kind of danger she was in. A sailor she recognized had brought their food—the one with the narrow hungry face who had stared at her on the deck. So long ago that seemed, but those foxy features were hard to forget. He had a thin mustache, she saw now, that drooped over his lip, and a tattoo snaking around his wrist from thumb to forearm. He had laid out the gruel, hard biscuit and water jug with exaggerated, mocking care on their bed platform and glanced furtively down the length of the ship's shadowed belly.

He turned to her then, sidled up until she was pressed against the curved sidewall of the cell. His tattooed hand reached out and grasped her curls—dirty curls they were now, but as bright and tumbled as ever—fingering them slowly, luxuriously, his lips spreading into an avid leer. She tried to shrink away, but there was nowhere to go.

"Get off her!" Luc shouted at the man—she heard Matthieu's shrill voice as well—and both boys rushed at the pirate. Matthieu grabbed at him from behind, trying to pull him backward, but Luc came in from the side, landing a hard blow in the crook of the man's arm that jerked it down and away from Madeleine's face. The tattooed fist opened, releasing her, and with a roar of anger the pirate rounded on Luc and struck. Madeleine saw blood streaming down Luc's chin, saw the pirate fling Matthieu like a ragdoll into his bunk, and didn't even realize she was yelling for help until a hand snaked forward and clamped over her mouth.

Luc might have suffered much worse than the split lip he now bore, Madeleine thought, if the uproar hadn't brought a new man running. She had seen this man turn sleeping sailors out of their hammocks and allocate the stores—he was some kind of officer, if pirates had such a thing. Twice again as big as her tormentor, with great slablike hands, he plucked the man off his feet and shook him like a naughty pup. An angry harangue poured from him, with gestures to Madeleine and a knotted fist brandished to underline his point. The Fox (Madeleine put the name to him without conscious thought as she recalled all that had happened) was surly but cowed, his eyes cast down. At last the officer had all but thrown him from the cell, slammed the door and locked it from the great iron ring of keys that swung at his hip.

The children had barely spoken after that, all three shaken by a new awareness of their helplessness. Madeleine prayed that the visit they received soon after had gone over Matthieu's head, but the memory of it gnawed at her. She understood, now, something of their fate.

The man had not bothered to come in but had addressed them through the iron rungs. "I am sent to you as I speak your tongue," he said, the words accented and exotic-sounding, but plain enough. He sounds like Yolenka, thought Madeleine, and the memory of their day at the docks was a flare of pain in her heart. "You"—his golden-brown eyes, almonds in a deeply tanned face, rested on Madeleine—"will not be touched. Boss say no man to have you. Worth better price at auction if you are fresh, yes?" The handsome face broke into a hard smile. "So, any man handle you, you scream loud. Yes?"

Madeleine managed a shaky nod. "Yes."

The man nodded, then jabbed a finger at Luc. "This means you too. You take this girl, we cut your throat. Is clear?"

Not waiting for a reply, he turned on his heel and disappeared up the hatch into the bright light that spilled in from the upper deck.

Better to be seasick than to think about those words "at auction," thought Madeleine. Better a storm to deal with, than another endless night drowning in memories and longings that did nothing but sharpen her grief. Better not to think about home.

CHAPTER TWELVE

EACH DAWN, THE SHIP WAS BATHED in a dreamy orange glow as the rising sun slanted through her ochre sails. Dominic was always up to see it. The captain had given up his tiny cabin for the two women, but the men slept cheek by jowl with the crew, tucked into rope hammocks. Only Derkh seemed to find them comfortable—it was the swell and roll of the ship in high water that gave him trouble.

Even in a feather bed, though, Dominic would have been restless. Their flurry of preparation and packing—Dominic's part had been to outfit the company with weaponry and wealth ("as much as possible, in gold," Yolenka had urged), while the others had been busy acquiring remedies and herbs, smithing tools, everything needed to sustain their disguises—had been full of purpose and promise. Once on board, though, time stood still. Dominic knew they were following his children as fast as possible, but it was not like land travel, where you could count the passing leagues in horse sweat and new vistas. Every day the scenery was the same: gray ocean without end. There was no sense of progress.

There was, at least, plenty to do. Yolenka had combed Blanchette market for the most gaudy silky fabrics she could find, and she gave lessons in Tarzine while she sewed what would evidently become her costume. Their progress varied—Dominic and Derkh managed to pick up a few words and phrases, while Féolan seemed to inhale words from the very air. Within a few days he was trying his skills out with the Tarzine crew. Dominic's years on the coast had given him a working knowledge of sailing, and he prowled the ship, observing the differences that made the Tarzine craft superior in power and stability to anything in the Basin lands. When the weather was fine and the deck relatively free, Dominic sparred with Derkh or Féolan. They all felt rusty and were glad of the chance to sharpen their fighting edge.

Mostly, he tried to plan. Even a rudimentary plan, cobbled together from their vast lack of information, seemed better than none. His mind chewed on it through the day and into the long wakeful nights. It had to, to fend off the terrible thoughts that lay always in wait for him—thoughts of his children, their fear and loneliness and misery.

Yolenka answered all his questions patiently, but when Dominic asked her to draw him a map she shook her head and stood abruptly.

"Is not my skill. Wait here."

It did not take her long. "Captain will see you after evening meal. Has maps of coastline, harbors, better knowledge of Turga than me. I translate."

His debt to this exotic woman, a complete stranger, loomed suddenly immense. Dominic reached up and grasped her hand as she turned to go.

"Yolenka, I don't know how we could have done this without you. I—"

She cut him off with a smile so brittle it hurt to see it.

"Slavers take my sister when I am ten years old, just beginning as dancer. I never see again. We take back your children. Then you thank me."

"Turga's stronghold cannot be entered by sea," translated Yolenka, as the captain pointed to a tightly enclosed bay at the south end of the country's western coast. "Is guarded at mouth, impossible." She held up a finger to forestall Dominic's dismay.

"But children are going here—to Baskir." The captain ran his finger north up the rugged coast, illustrated with high cliffs along much of its length. "Is stupid for Turga to go first to his own land, then to slave auction by road. No—he sail straight to Baskir. Is big harbor, big market. Many ships coming and going. We land there, is easy."

Is easy. If only it were true, thought Gabrielle. For one moment, as they clustered around the captain's map, their quest had seemed a simple matter of sailing to the right place.

Well, she was happy to leave the strategizing to Dominic and the others. Gabrielle's business was with the children. Her mind never left them, as if her constant thought could keep them safe. She saw the pain and worry behind Dominic's nervous energy. They were her feelings too.

"Can you send your thoughts out after them, Féolan?" she asked. Elves, she knew, could touch a friend's spirit with love or strength.

Féolan looked up from his *lythra*. He had been rehearsing with Yolenka—an impatient taskmaster—and was trying to fix in his head and fingers the strange melodies and rhythms she had sung for him. From the sheltered corner he and Gabrielle had found on the deck the sound floated out and hovered, stirring and mournful, between the dark water and the night's first stars.

He shook his head sadly. "They are too far, love, and our connection too faint. I cannot find them."

So he had tried. How she loved him for that. Pulling her shawl closer about her, she leaned against his warm back. The evening was cooling off quickly, but neither was in a hurry to exchange the open sky for the cramped lower deck, redolent as it was of unwashed bodies and the fish oil used to preserve the planking.

"Play on, then, my troubadour." And she returned to the prayer that played over and over in her heart: Let them be safe. Let them find comfort. Let them have hope.

CHAPTER THIRTEEN

MATTHIEU HAD BEEN THINKING. Madeleine hadn't said one word about it, but he knew she had heard the word too. *Auction.* He knew what that meant. It meant they would be sold, like horses.

When he was little, maybe, he would have imagined an auction for nice families who didn't have children of their own. Not now. No, he would be no better than a plow horse or sheepdog, a beast existing only to work and obey. And Madeleine…It would be worse for Madeleine.

But that one word had given him an idea.

"Maddy, listen. I think we should try to get that guy back, the one who speaks Krylaise, and tell him who we are."

Madeleine was bent over with her hair tumbled forward, scratching the back of her scalp with both hands. It brought only temporary relief from the tiny, bloodsucking lice that infested all of them, but the sensation was glorious while it lasted. She flipped the dirty curls back and sat on her hands before they moved on to claw at her wrists and ankles.

"Why?" she asked dully. "What difference will it make?" She was different since that man had spoken to them, thought Matthieu. Sometimes it seemed like she was only half there.

"They're going to sell us, right?" Madeleine's eyes shifted away at his words, but her tiny reluctant nod acknowledged them. "So they're only after money. Our parents would pay to get us back— and you too," he added, bringing Luc into the family with a wave of his hand. "They'd pay more than anybody! So if we tell them who we are, that they can just sell us back, maybe they will!"

Her blue eyes grew round. "Oh, Matthieu, I wonder...Except they would have to bring us all the way back."

"So we promise them even more money!"

Madeline nodded, slowly. "I can't see any reason not to try." She flashed him a smile, his old Maddy back, hope kindling her features. Then she grew serious and lowered her voice. "There's another thing. We don't want the pirates to know they may be trying to follow us. Don't say anything about that."

"The rescue" had become a little fiction they were careful to keep alive, though neither had mentioned it in days. It was the storm, Matthieu thought, that had put an end to any real hope. Clinging to Madeleine in the dark as the ship plunged and lurched and spray cascaded down the hatch, he had begun to grasp the vastness of the ocean and the invisibility of their passage. There was nothing for his father, or the best tracker in the world, to follow.

Luc broke in. "Your family must be some rich if they could buy you back." He was eyeing them queerly, as though they had turned into strangers.

"My father will be king of Verdeau," Matthieu announced. It was not a boast, exactly, but he could not keep the pride from his voice. Luc would be impressed, even if the Tarzines were not.

But he had not intended to make his new friend grovel. Luc's face became the picture of dismay. Then he dropped his head nearly to his waist, his fist clamped to the rough forelock that hung over his eyes.

"Beggin' yer pardon," he muttered. "I didn't know. I wouldn't have made so free with ye—"

"Luc, stop." It was Madeleine, looking as upset as Luc did. She walked over and pulled down his arm. "Please, stand up. Look at me."

It was hard for him, but there was no evading those round blue eyes. "It was exactly right, what you said when we met. It means nothing here, being noble-born or not. And now that I've met you, I wish it meant nothing back home." She took a deep breath, and her pale cheeks colored. "I'm proud to have you for a friend—Matthieu too, I'm sure." Madeleine fixed Matthieu with the same demanding stare.

He nodded, hard. Luc had got his lip split open defending Maddy, had held Matthieu's shoulders while he puked into that vile bucket. They were in this together.

TWO DAYS OF CLAMORING, entreating and gesticulating every time a sailor passed near finally brought the interpreter back to the children's cell.

He listened with undisguised impatience and gave a dismissive laugh as Madeleine laid out their proposal. "Is pretty plan. But you need very rich father to pay Turga his price, plus return trip!"

Madeleine drew herself up and spoke now with quiet emphasis. They had agreed to save this trump card for last.

"He *is* very rich. He is the king."

The broad back, already turned toward them, froze. It hovered, undecided, for a second. Then the man faced Madeleine once more. His eyes narrowed as he searched her face, and she did her best to stand tall under his scrutiny.

"You lie about this, Turga makes you very sorry."

"I do not lie. My brother here is heir to the throne." The words startled Madeleine as she spoke them. She had never before thought of Matthieu as—well, as anything but a kid.

Another hard stare, a curt nod, and the man was striding down the gallery.

Time crawled by. Madeleine's stomach became more and more jumpy as she weighed the possibilities: Would he dismiss their claim? Present it to Turga? Matthieu became so restless she wanted to yell at him. And then more time, a crushing silence, hope bleeding away with every passing moment until Matthieu, kicking the bulkhead with a curse, threw himself onto the platform and burst into harsh sobs. Madeleine felt her own throat close up and the hot tears spill. She cried, helplessly, into her hands.

The touch was so light, so hesitant, that she didn't notice it at first. Luc's hand on her shoulder, skittish as a deer. "Hush, now," he whispered as though to a baby.

She had never needed a friend more. She leaned into his skinny chest and wept.

"MADDY, HE'S COMING!"

What passed for dinner was over, and the light from the hatchways had dimmed to gray when their interpreter returned.

"Turga thanks you for your offer." The formal tone was confusing. Was it serious? A mockery? The children held their breath.

"But is no good. Here he has gold in his fist, easy, safe. There—

is long trip, no guarantees and at end maybe more fighting. Not worth trouble."

The man's gaze sharpened on Madeleine, became somehow cold and hot at once so that she colored to the roots of her hair. The smile was tight, wolfish. "You make Turga happy. Young princess is sure to bring top price!"

CHAPTER FOURTEEN

IN THE DARK CONFINES of the captain's berth, Gabrielle tossed and muttered, trapped in an evil dream. *She couldn't breathe. A gray fog seeped over her face, oozing into her mouth. Thick wooly tendrils slid down her throat. She gagged and thrashed against them, but each smothered sucking breath pulled the dark miasma farther into her windpipe. The gray fog filled her. It was killing her.*

Even in her sleep Gabrielle knew this was a True Dream. She had learned much about dreaming in her years with the Elves, learned to tell the fragmented nonsense of her mind's fancies and fears from the powerful eye of true dreaming. She had learned to let the dream play out with a delicate awareness that did not jar her into wakefulness. But this time she could not do it. She fought against the dream, fought, as it seemed, for her life.

With a gasp and a retching cough she wrenched herself from sleep's grasp. Shaky with the clammy horror that still clung to her, she groped for Féolan and found only the clinkered wood of the ship's hull. Now she felt the crest and fall of the ship over the waves and remembered the narrow berth that was her bed on this journey. Only Yolenka shared the tiny cabin with her, and she slept on undisturbed.

Gabrielle considered waking her but settled for lighting the lamp. Like nearly everything else in the cabin, it was fixed in place, settled firmly into a wall bracket. It made a small wavering pool of yellow light—enough, she hoped, to chase some of the chill from her heart.

There would be no going back to sleep, not for a while. Gabrielle climbed into her berth and set her back against the curved wall. She needed to think about her dream. The gods of light and darkness knew how little she relished the prospect, but since it haunted her anyway, she might as well seek some understanding of it.

The meaning was not necessarily literal, this much she knew. The foreboding she felt, though—and she realized, now, that a growing uneasiness had been stalking her all that day—*that* could be trusted. The danger was real. But the danger might not be hers; dreamers often felt the dream's message within themselves, and as a healer she was more prone than most to take on another's pain or sorrow. The dream might be about her, or someone she knew, or a more general warning of...what?

Gabrielle shivered and pulled her blanket close about her. Again in her mind's eye the gray fog blanketed her body.

A light knock.

"Gabrielle?"

Féolan. Silent in her bare feet, Gabrielle opened the cabin door before Féolan was sure he had been heard.

"I'm so glad you're here."

"Are you all right, love? I woke up thinking of you."

More than thinking, Gabrielle guessed. If he had reached his mind out to her—and he surely had—he would have felt her panic.

"I had a terrible dream, Féolan, a True Dream."

Yolenka stirred in her sleep, and Gabrielle pitched her voice down.

"It was so frightening, and the only sense I can make of it is that it's something bad."

Féolan wrapped his arms around her and held her close and still. Gabrielle let his warm, steadying strength seep into her. It was as real and certain as the rocking of the ship under her feet. "Thank you," she whispered.

"Least I can do. Do you want to talk it through or leave it till morning? They say dark dreams fare better in daylight."

Gabrielle nodded into his chest. "Could you sit with me a while, do you think? There isn't really any room for you, but…"

They did find a hazy sort of sleep, eventually, slumped side by side against the wall with Féolan's legs trailing onto the floor. And that was how Yolenka found them, in the narrow shafts of light that brought morning to the captain's cabin.

"Good day, little lovebirds! Time to wake up your eyes!"

The voice was amused, brash and worlds away from any dark dream. Gabrielle opened her eyes to a wide knowing grin.

"Is good you are healer. You are two pained necks and twisted-up backs today, yes?"

SOMETHING WAS WRONG with Luc.

Turga's rejection of their offer had been devastating, yet Madeleine did not sink back into the dull despair that had sucked at her when she first realized their fate. They had made a good try, something with a real chance of success. If one was possible, why not another? And if the children had been able to think up a worthwhile plan, who was to say their father could not do so as well? It was a slim enough hope, but Madeleine was determined to keep hold of it.

Luc, though, became tense and silent. They had come to rely on the older boy, Madeleine realized; his sturdy friendship helped them cope with everything from seasickness to runaway fear. But that night he did not speak a word or even look at them. He paced and scratched until bedtime, and then twitched and muttered through the long black hours. Madeleine awoke in the morning—what passed for morning in the shadowy hold—to find Luc sitting propped against the bulkhead with his arms wrapped round his knees, his face set, eyes starey and wild.

"Luc, what is it?" She wondered if he would answer, or even hear her.

"I won't be any man's slave!" The words burst out of him, hot and emphatic. He shook his head, underlining his refusal. "I can work hard; it ain't that. I been on my pa's boat since I could pull up a crab trap. But to be owned like a dog, beaten or fed at another man's say-so…no. No, I'd rather be dead."

"But, Luc—" Madeleine closed her mouth. He didn't need her to point out that they weren't being offered a choice.

"I'm going to escape, Maddy." He leaned forward, serious and intent. "Soon as we land, first chance I get, I'm taking off."

"I am too!" Matthieu was sitting up, hair tousled from his blankets, face shining with enthusiasm.

"Good," Luc agreed. "We should all three go together. It will take them more by surprise, and there's a better chance of at least one getting away."

Madeleine looked at Matthieu's eager features, and her heart sank. Luc's talk made Matthieu feel courageous and strong, and that was better than helplessness, she knew that. But she knew too that their brave escape plans would soon butt up against reality. And reality was this: If, by some remote miracle, they managed to get away from Turga's army of pirates without being killed or recaptured, they would be lost in a foreign land, with no idea where to go and no way to speak to a soul. They might as well plan to sprout wings and fly.

THE LAST TRACES of daylight lent a sheen to the waters of Baskir harbor as the ship eased slowly toward the wharf. Turga took no pleasure in the golden evening. He far preferred to make harbor before midday, with time to unload his cargo and get it safely stored and under guard before his crew got their pay and shore leave. He was not about to unload a ship in the dark; it was far too difficult to track the goods, too tempting for the men to pilfer as they worked. And he knew the limits of leadership better than to try to keep the men on board through the night after two months at sea.

No, the cargo would have to stay on board, with a few hand-picked and well-paid men to guard it. The others would tumble off the ship and into the town, hungry for drink and food and women, and be in poor shape for work on the morrow.

There would be no drunken revels for Turga nor women either, until they reached his stronghold. A man did not stay warlord long by dropping his trousers in a rival's territory. Grindor grew rich off Baskir's trade and would not discourage visiting merchants by indulging in outright robbery—but what happened in the streets at night was another matter.

He let his thoughts play over the plunder he had piled in the ship's belly. A disappointing haul, he would have said, but for the children. Those last two had been a lucky find, and the news of their royalty even luckier. Were they bluffing? No matter, Turga decided. Bathe and dress that girl properly, and with her glorious hair and startling round eyes she would look every inch the foreign princess.

CHAPTER FIFTEEN

ATTHIEU HAD CURLED into his ragged blanket and fallen asleep soon after their evening meal. Madeleine was thinking about joining him—they all felt weak and tired now, worn out from the toxic mix of fear and inactivity. When she was sleeping, she could forget about the itching and the smell and the constant gnawing upset in her stomach.

Then they heard orders called out from the deck above, a flurry of hurried footsteps overhead, the crackle of flapping sail, and the ship suddenly slowed. Luc's head pricked up like a hound on scent.

"They're trimming the sails."

"What does that mean?"

"They're reducing the amount of sail so the ship goes slower," he explained. "Taking some right down, or maybe folding 'em up smaller. It's for rough weather, or..."

His eyes, scared now under his rough bangs, met hers. "Or for coming into harbor."

Madeleine's belly became a live thing with teeth and claws, icy and hot and liquid. The fetid air was too thick to breathe—her chest heaved with the effort of drawing it in, but even so she was choked and dizzy. All this time, the deepest part of her had not believed it would come to this—that she would actually arrive in this hostile land, be torn away from her brother, exist only to serve the whim of the highest bidder. Now the pretense crumpled, and the scrape of the oars being fitted into the oarlocks, the jerky rhythm of their strokes, underscored her terror. This was no dream. Her father had not come. Time had run out.

Then Luc's arms were around her, strong despite the quaver in his own voice. "There, Maddy. There now."

She wrapped her arms tight and clung on. But though the comfort of his lean warmth helped her breath come easier, the swirling thoughts would not still: She would never see her mama grow old, never see Sylvain grow to a man. Never see the sun rise over the Avine River or ride through the Chênier hills. Never have a boyfriend or husband of her own, but only masters who—

Madeleine raised her head and fixed Luc with blue eyes that blazed with equal parts fear and determination.

"Luc—kiss me."

"*What* say?" Luc's shock would have made her laugh in a happier time and place. Not now. She was fierce with urgency.

"I mean it. Just one time I want to kiss a boy because I choose to. Because I like him, not because he bought me. Please—"

She didn't have to ask again. His lips were chapped—hers too—and they both stank. She didn't care. They kissed each other for a long time, tenderly, sadly, and when they drew apart the scrabbly panic had receded. It was still there, but so was her own strength.

She took a deep breath and stepped back. "I better wake Matthieu."

THE SHIP MADE berth in a flurry of commands and brisk activity. The children listened and waited, their tension ratcheting tighter minute by minute. They had hated this ship, but now they were terrified to leave it. When the men began pouring down the hatchways, they were sure they would be taken—but no one so much as glanced their way. The crew were busy at their bunks—rummaging through their kits, stuffing purses with coin, donning bright neck scarves or less filthy tunics—and then they were gone. Night and silence descended on the ship.

"Will they just leave us here?" asked Madeleine.

"Maybe just till morning," suggested Luc. "The men—"

"The men have gone drinking." Matthieu jumped in, relieved, Madeleine saw, to have some diversion for his mind. "Remember what Uncle Tristan told us, Maddy, that the harbor tavern keepers were happy when Tarzine ships arrived? They always eat and drink lots—"

Matthieu's voice stopped abruptly and he turned away, his shoulders hunched as though fending off a blow. Madeleine understood. Matthieu adored his uncle, hung on his every word and exploit. With the mere mention of his name, Tristan had sprung as vividly into her mind as if he stood in the cramped cell beside them, and with him came all the other people she loved and longed for. Then they crumbled to dust and were gone.

It was hot below decks—they were on land again in high summer, and the deepening night was thick and muggy. It was late when Madeleine fell into uneasy half-sleep, later still when a commotion on deck jolted her awake, her heart tripping like a frightened bird's. But it was not morning—the open hatchways were black still—and no one came for them. Now and then a group of men made their way to the berths by lamp or torchlight, rummaged with their things and climbed back up the hatches.

The men were silent and their faces, when the flames caught them, were grim.

She shook the boys awake. "Something's happening."

Angry words sounded on deck, a proper tongue-lashing to hear it, and shouted commands, a flurry of footsteps, the scrape of oars in the oarlocks. The ship moved, almost imperceptibly at first and then in the jerky rhythm of hard rowing. Some time later, they heard the crinkle and flap of sails unfurling, and then felt the ship list as the night breeze tugged at the sails.

"We're heading out," Luc muttered. "I don't get it." He was a voice in the blackness, nothing more.

Madeleine's mind was doing a complicated skittish dance, circling around the flare of hope that she was afraid to grab hold of.

But Matthieu did it for her. "He changed his mind, that Turga. What else could it be? He's taking us back home for ransom. That's why the crew's mad—they thought they were getting a holiday, and now they're back to work!" His hand groped for hers, caught it, squeezed hard. She squeezed back, unable to speak around the hard ball of tears that had grown in her throat. She wanted so badly for Matthieu to be right. But she knew too much now, and she didn't believe it.

IT HAD NOT yet been fully dark when Turga's first mate, Zhirak, had returned to the ship, his expression uneasy. "It's bad, boss. Half of Baskir's closed up—Grindor just ordered the plague flags hung out. It's the Gray Veil, spreading fast if you believe the wenches at Puka's. Of course, *he'd* be open for business if the place was on fire."

Turga cursed, his mind already racing ahead.

"The auction?"

"Closed. You know it hits young ones the worst. They don't even want 'em in the holding pens. No one will buy a slave that might spread sickness through the house and be dead in a week."

Children made up more than half of most auction offerings. Buyers considered them more trainable than adults, and better value in terms of potential years of service. But Zhirak was right— in this particular circumstance, youth was a liability.

"Bring the men back." There was no time to lose. Turga had seen the Veil at work long ago, seen his small brother whistle and gasp to breathe around the evil coating that spread over the back of his throat and filled up his tiny airways. The lad had lived, but plenty in their village had not.

"Sir? They're all over town by now."

"Find them!" The command was roared. "Take the three who came back with you and the two above-deck guards and scour the town. Haul their arses back to the ship, and demon-fire take you if you fail."

The startled men scrambled toward the catwalk.

They would sail to Rath Turga at first light and keep the children there until the epidemic died down and the markets re-opened. And he would promise gold to his own patron god, the axe-wielder Kiar, if the Great Hewer would only ensure that no invisible unwanted guest came aboard with the returning crew.

CHAPTER SIXTEEN

TURGA'S STRONGHOLD WAS AN IMPRESSIVE SIGHT. The deep bay was nearly a lagoon, so tightly did the two craggy outcrops of land enclose it. The children did not see the ship's journey through those straits, but they heard the braying horns that announced Turga's arrival.

This time they were taken off the ship soon after it nudged up to the quay. Matthieu fought to keep hold of Madeleine, but they were pried apart by the three burly pirates who came for them. The bright morning stabbed at his eyes and made them water as he was thrust through the hatch and into the light—yet to feel the warm sun beating down and breathe sweet air again was lovely beyond belief. He squinted up at the massive building that brooded over the harbor.

It seemed to grow out of the high cliff it was built upon, a squat, nearly windowless hulk of red stone enclosed by a matching wall. Smaller than Castle DesChênes, it was a good deal more imposing. It did not seem like a place where anyone would live.

"It's a fortress, Maddy," Matthieu breathed, impressed despite his fear. "Like in the general's stories of the old heroes." Before she could answer they were pulled along, off the ship and along the jetty to a broad, hard-packed dirt road that skirted wide of the cliff-face and then snaked uphill to Turga's stronghold.

It was a long climb up to the fortress. The children were kept in single file, each escorted by a guard and flanked by the handful of crew members who were not assigned to unloading the ship. The sun was hot on Matthieu's head and back, though it was not yet midmorning. The land that stretched out beyond the road had a dry, baked look, the vegetation sparse and dusty. Walking felt strange after so long at sea, and Matthieu's legs tired quickly. Even the guards, he noticed, were breathing hard by the time they were halfway to the gate. Luc stumbled in front of him, loose stones and dust spilling down from the scrape of his shoe. The guard, who had let go of Luc's arm to avoid falling himself, bent over to help the boy up. But Luc twisted around, kicked out hard to the pit of the guard's stomach and was on his feet and running into the brush.

He did it! The thought was a shout of triumph in Matthieu's head, a lightning bolt of excitement. But Luc hadn't made twenty paces before three pirates sprinted after him. They ran him down like a rabbit, and though he twisted and turned to escape their grasp, at the end he was sent sprawling into the hard-packed earth. Matthieu's heart sank as Luc's guard, recovered now, made his way down the slope to where Luc lay pinned. The man stood, expressionless, as Luc hoisted up to his knees and started to his feet. Then his heavy booted foot swung back.

Matthieu heard Madeleine cry out behind him as the boot caught Luc under his ribs and lifted him into the air. A moment later he was slung between two pirates and hauled back to the road. He looks like a fish, thought Matthieu, the image absurd and horrifying at once. Luc's mouth gaped in a fruitless attempt to suck air as the guards shouldered him back into place. Finally, when it seemed to Matthieu his friend must breathe or suffocate, Luc lifted his head and Matthieu heard the long gasping rush as his wind returned.

Matthieu raised his eyes once more to the tall enclosure now looming and the thick red walls of the fortress beyond. He had been stupid to imagine such a place had anything to do with heroes and adventures and old tales. It was a prison, nothing more.

DOMINIC GRIPPED THE handrail and stared across the wide bay to the dark blurry jumble that was Baskir. Could the wretched ship go no faster? The town crept into focus more slowly than his frayed nerves could stand. His children could be on the auction block even now, sold out from under his very nose, while the ship dawdled into port.

It was a large town with an extensive harbor—he could see that now. It sat nestled into gentle green banks, but Dominic could see to the south the low bare mountains that marked the beginning of the dry upland plateau known as the badlands. This town, Yolenka had told him, marked the unproclaimed border where the rule of law lost its hold completely and the warlords held sway. The slave auction was just one of the illegal activities that thrived in Baskir, and its overlord, Grindor, was smart enough to ensure that wealthy visitors from the northern settlements were left to do their business in safety. "Many rich families in the north, even in the Emperor's own city, have slaves," Yolenka had told them with obvious disgust. "They say, 'Oh, is my young servant, is daughter of my maid,' and everyone knows what is truth but they say nothing. And the warlords fill their pockets and grow strong with the gold of these people."

They were closer now—the network of wharves reaching far out into the water, though with fewer ships at berth than Dominic would expect from so much docking space. His stomach clenched in a roil of doubt. This was not his style, sneaking around, adopting false roles and an innocent facade. Who on earth would believe he was married to a Tarzine dancer? He clung to the hope that they would be able to make a straightforward raid on the slave house without need for such playacting.

Black banners flew at the end of each pier and from the higher buildings along the shorefront. That certainly seemed at odds with Yolenka's taste for color. He tapped her shoulder, pointing them out.

"What do the flags represent, Yolenka? Are they the city's standard, or do they proclaim a warlord's territory?"

Yolenka squinted into the wind. Dominic had been around her enough now to recognize the curse that escaped her. She turned to him, her face stricken. But her reply was drowned out by a loud cry from one of the sailors. He was pointing to shore, yelling the same Tarzine word over and over. Soon all the men around them took up the refrain.

"What is it, Yolenka?"

They all clustered around her now, anxious to understand, but the din of the sailors made it impossible to hear until Derkh pointed to the hatch and led them to the relative quiet of the belowdecks.

"Is warning to stay away." Yolenka shook her head, words for once eluding her.

"Is…sign of sickness, bad sickness that goes all through city. Is danger sign."

"Plague?" asked Gabrielle sharply. "Some sort of plague?" There had been no plague in the Basin during her lifetime, but she had heard of the terrible illnesses that could spread over a land, leaving behind more dead than could be decently buried.

Yolenka shrugged. "I not know this word, plague. Is sickness that goes fast from one to other person, goes everywhere. They are closing city to keep it inside."

ONLY WHEN THE ship was turned around and heading back out to sea would the captain sit down to discuss a new plan. Braving the plague flags and entering Baskir was not an option he would entertain.

"The children may not be there, in any case," suggested Féolan. "Not if the banners were up when Turga arrived."

"The captain say we had fast crossing," added Yolenka. "We are not more than two days behind."

"So if Turga sailed here and saw the banners, what would he do?" asked Dominic.

"Go to his stronghold and wait where is safe," said Yolenka. "Wait till slave market opens."

"But we can't sail to—what is it called? Rath Turga? The captain said so."

The captain bent over his map, jabbed with a brown weathered finger. Yolenka nodded.

"If it is open, no sickness, we can land here," she translated. "Niz Hana. Is small harbor, only a few deep...ah...tie up places. Hire cart, mule, travel to Rath Turga by road, is not so far. Captain waits with ship."

"How long?" asked Derkh.

The captain considered. "Seven days should be enough," Yolenka translated. "He waits ten. But if black flags go up in Niz Hana, he leaves and we are left."

CHAPTER SEVENTEEN

"Matthieu, Madeleine...I'm sorry."
Madeleine looked across the cell to where Luc sat
hunched on his iron bedstead, elbows on knees. He
was scraped and scuffed everywhere, blood drying on his chin
and palms and forearms. She winced at the thought of the bruise
that must be spreading under his shirt and hoped no bones had
been broken.

"Sorry for what?"

Luc glanced up through his rough fringe of hair, then away.
"I said we'd all go together. But the sight of this building...And
then I saw a chance—and I just kind of panicked and ran.

"I'm sorry," he said again. "I should have stuck with you."

"Luc, listen." Madeleine looked at Luc, but her message was
even more for Matthieu. She knew now what she wanted to say
about the notion of escape.

"There was no chance for us to all get away at once. There
probably never will be. And there wasn't really a chance for you,
either."

"There was. My legs were just weak from bein' cooped up for
so long. Otherwise, I could've outrun 'em."

Madeleine shook her head impatiently. "Even if you did. Then
what? Where would you go?"

Luc shrugged. "Down the coast. I know how to fish. I'd find some guy who could use a hand."

He had some kind of plan, at least. "It's a good idea," Madeleine conceded. "But without a word of Tarzine, you couldn't even speak to anyone, or get any sense of whether they were inclined to take you in or take you back."

Luc glared at her. "What do you suggest then? Just give up?"

"No! But bide your time." Madeleine gestured to their leg chains. "Wherever we end up, it won't be as guarded as this. They'll have to let you out to work. Work hard, do what you're told, let your master relax and start to trust you. Learn the language and how things work here. *Then* when a chance comes along, you'll be ready."

Luc set his face and said nothing, but Matthieu was nodding in agreement. "If I get away, I'll come look for you. Both of you."

"No, Matthieu." This part was hard to say. Madeleine took a deep breath and plunged on. "If you get away, I want you to get home. Maybe father could pay a Tarzine merchant to search for us and buy us back. But if you try, you're too likely to be recaptured. Don't do it."

Could she really follow her own advice, Madeleine wondered—escape and leave Matthieu behind? It was unthinkable. But then, so was nearly everything about her life now.

GOLD IN THE PALM of the harbormaster of Niz Hana for the privilege of making berth. More gold for their safe passage through town and for directions to a carter who could supply them with travel gear. A ridiculous amount of gold for the brightly painted tented wagon Yolenka pronounced "perfect" and the mule (plus feed) to pull it. Dominic understood now why she had insisted they come laden with wealth. He shifted his weight on the hard platform that was the driver's seat, trying to fit himself into the depression worn into the wood by some previous owner. He flicked the long reins impatiently (and without effect) over the plodding mule, and wondered yet again if this elaborate charade was not just foolishness.

"Shouldn't we have horses?" Derkh had protested. "We can hardly make a getaway with one mule."

He had voiced Dominic's thoughts precisely, but Yolenka shook her head in adamant insistence.

"Some traders, yes, are rich enough for wagons and horses both. Top craftsmen, demanded by kings. Men with names. Not little traveling bands like this. No one will believe."

She noted Dominic's troubled frown.

"You have army, then yes, ride down on Turga and fight. Maybe you win where others fail. No army? Then you need way to get inside. Worry about 'getaway' after."

"Dom."

Gabrielle's hand rested light on his arm, joggling in the same mule-cart rhythm that rocked his body. Her green eyes held his in that direct warm gaze that seemed to look right into his soul.

"You made the right decision."

Her offer to ride up front with him had been more than casual, Dominic realized. Gabrielle had played little part in their preparations so far, but Dom was suddenly very glad to have her along. Just her quiet presence renewed his hope and courage. She smiled at him now.

"Sneaking around in disguise goes against your grain, I know. But this is Yolenka's country, and you are right to put your trust in her knowledge. We'll find a way to get out again."

CHAPTER EIGHTEEN

THE BOYS LOOKED SO DIFFERENT with their hair cut short, thought Madeleine. Luc seemed older, the lean firm planes of his face more prominent. Matthieu, though—the close crop exposed all his childish roundness, the brown trusting eyes and soft cheeks. She could look at him now and see him at five, a chubby charming pest, and the memory brought the sting of tears to her eyes.

"How come they left your hair long?" Matthieu was rubbing his hand back and forth over the dark carpet on his head, fascinated with its bristly softness.

Madeleine knew why. Because exotic foreign princess slaves sell better with long red-blond curls, that was why. She also knew why she and Luc had been chained by the ankle to their heavy iron bedsteads, on opposite sides of the room so that at the full length of the chain they could touch hands, but no more. Because exotic foreign princess slaves sell better when no other man has touched them. Still, for now they were better off than on the ship, and for that she was grateful.

The room, with only a narrow slit of a window, a single lamp and a solid wood door, was every bit as dark as the hold of the ship had been. And it was hot. But it was dry and clean and, blessedly, so were they.

Matthieu had looked so scared when, only a short while after they had climbed the narrow stone stairs to their cell, guards had come and taken him and Luc away. This is it, Madeleine had thought, her heart a frozen stone in her chest. The last I will ever see him.

Then she had been taken as well, by two silent armed women, to an outdoor enclosure where her clothes were stripped off her and tossed onto a fire and she was scrubbed from head to foot with a stinging pungent soap that made her pale skin bloom into red blotches. And her hair—no wonder the boys' hair had been cut! After coating her head in a thick oily concoction that reeked of herbs and lamp oil, it had taken the women most of the afternoon to comb, with painstaking thoroughness, the bugs and nits out of each strand of hair and finally to wash out the greasy mess. When at last she was brought back, Matthieu had hurtled into her arms. Madeleine understood what he didn't say: He had thought she was gone for good.

"Why did they bother to clean us up like this?" Madeleine was changing the subject, but she truly wondered. The long tunics they had been given were rough but clean, and so were the thin pallets on their bedsteads. Her skin and scalp felt almost sunburned from its harsh treatment, but already the fierce constant itching of wrists and ankles and neck she had endured on the ship was subsiding.

Luc shrugged. "Lots of those pirates were out there getting cleaned up too. They didn't burn their clothes, but they dumped 'em all into big vats of boiling water, and they scrubbed 'emselves raw just like us. Maybe Turga doesn't like bedbugs in his house."

A heavy tread and the sound of a key opening the door's padlock interrupted them. As the door was pulled back, a thick aroma wafted into the room. Meat and spices—something sharp that licked at the nostrils—and a sweet fruity…Madeleine's mouth filled with saliva and her stomach cramped sharply. She knew she must have the same hawklike intensity on her own face that she saw on Luc's and Matthieu's as they stared at the large tray carried in by yet another stranger. They barely noticed him leaving as they clustered around it.

"What is this stuff?" asked Luc. It didn't look like anything from home; that was certain. Fist-sized packets of something wrapped in steamed leaves of some kind, heaps of a tiny bright-yellow grain, shriveled orange-red chunks that Madeleine hoped were dried fruit, greens so dark they were almost black.

Matthieu bent over the tray and took a deep fervent sniff.

"It's food, Luc. Real food that a person would actually want to eat."

There was very little talk after that. They fell on their dinner, and until it was gone Madeleine did not think once about slave auctions or home or the chain on her ankle. She just ate.

BREAKFAST WAS NOT so sumptuous, but it was wholesome and plentiful: bread and fruit and a bowl of creamy-looking stuff that was too tart for pudding, too liquid for cheese and too cold for soup. They debated over this for some time until Matthieu solved the problem by scooping a generous layer onto his bread and wolfing it down. It was good that way, they agreed—odd, but good.

But as the day wore on, the novelty of being clean and well-fed was no longer enough to fend off reality. Good food, however cheering, would not change their fate. The chain rubbed and dragged at Madeleine's leg, no matter how she sat or lay, making an angry red weal around her ankle. The dim shadows pressed on her—she was smothered by this constant confinement in constricted dark spaces. And the future was still a lurking terror. Madeleine fingered a tress of golden hair, let it twine around her finger like a morning glory. It would turn to the light like an eager plant, if only there were any. Her hair had felt rough and dry after the delousing, but that morning one of the silent women had come again and dressed it with a light fragrant oil and then brushed it into glossy health. She had made Madeleine rub the oil into her skin too. It was not a kindness; Madeleine understood that. They just wanted to keep her beautiful.

When the sun had lowered in the sky enough to pierce directly through the window, Madeleine stood and walked into the stream of light. She wanted to bathe her face in sunshine, to let the light penetrate and warm the dark hollow of her heart. But the chain brought her up short, so that she could not turn into the light, but could only stand with her back to the window and let the sunshine play on her head and shoulders.

That was where she stood when the key grated harshly in the lock and the door was pulled open.

Madeleine jumped, startled by the sudden intrusion. She had heard no footsteps—and a quick look confirmed that Matthieu and Luc were also taken by surprise.

Then she saw who it was, and her stomach tightened into a knot of fear.

SHE COULD NOT know it, but for one brief moment when he entered the cell, the sight of Madeleine made the man known as Rhus doubt his course. Backlit in a shaft of brilliance, her hair a golden blazing halo, she looked to his fevered brain more like a spirit messenger of the sun than a slave girl. But then she took a hasty step away, and the fire dimmed back into human hair and flesh.

It was a risky move, stealing the key and coming here, but he was done for anyway—had been the moment he hurried off with that painted whore instead of heeding Zhirak's shouted recall to the ship. His tyrant uncle could rail at him all he liked, as he had railed at Rhus's late return. It made no difference to him now. In the meantime, Rhus meant to satisfy his appetites while he still could. And high on his list of appetites was this girl, who had caught his eye her first day on board and tormented his thoughts ever since.

Sliding his long knife from its sheath, he backed first the young lad and then the meddlesome older boy into their respective corners. He laid the blade flat and hard against their lips and mimed the cut throat he would give them if they made a sound. Then he swaggered back to the young miss, pressed now against the wall as if it could swallow her up.

Oh, and wasn't she the pretty thing, pale and delicate as a new moon and hair to drive a man wild. Only the wide blue eyes unnerved him, like the sky itself accusing him.

She'll close 'em soon enough, he thought, and felt his lips flare across his face in a greedy smile. Her mouth he would close for her.

MADELEINE COULD NOT KEEP herself from shrinking away from the Fox, but she knew it was useless. She could go nowhere, do nothing. She didn't even have the option of trying to fight back—it was Matthieu he would kill, not her, and that was a risk she could not take.

The man's eyes swept her up and down, glittery and wild, and the narrow lips peeled back from his teeth.

Like he wants to eat me, thought Madeleine. Her stomach lurched, disgust and fear rising like vomit up her throat.

She didn't mean to make that pathetic frightened mew as the tattooed hand reached for her, but the sound slipped out and that was what spurred on Matthieu.

"Stop it! Leave her be!" he yelled and launched himself at the Fox.

"Matthieu, don't!" Madeleine shouted, but the Fox was faster. He had Matthieu in the corner, his knife pinned across his throat. Matthieu's eyes were huge, his face drained of color.

"Matthieu, you must stay quiet." Madeleine forced herself to talk quietly, though her voice shook with brimming tears. "Whatever happens, don't move. Don't say anything." *Don't look*, she wanted to add, but the Fox was already turning back to her, his sharp cheekbones flushed red with anger, sweat starting out on his forehead.

He slid his knife lingeringly alongside her throat and nestled it behind her ear before plunging his other hand into her hair, grabbing onto a fistful and pulling her hard against his body.

He trembled as he pressed against her and fumbled at her clothes. The hard hands, when they found and grasped at the bare skin under her loose tunic, were so hot she felt seared. His face too, seemed to throb with heat against her cheek. He pushed her to the ground, and when she resisted he slapped her, hard and fast, on the side of her head, and then brought his face so close they were nose to nose. Breathing heavily, he pressed the knife into her neck as he barked out an angry command. A stream of spittle escaped his lips. Madeleine smelled something awful on his breath, something swampy and putrid, and she gagged and flinched back.

Luc's voice shattered the air. Not bothering with words, he screamed. It cut through the despairing silence in the cell and blared like a shrieking trumpet into the hallway. Madeleine heard him suck in a breath, and then the clarion blared again, louder than any voice she had ever heard.

Blared, and held, and was cut short into a bubbly gurgle, and was gone. Only Matthieu's voice, a strangled bleating whimper, disturbed the room.

No. Please, great gods, any god, please no. Turning her head to look was like fighting a strong ocean current. How could it take so much effort and will, simply to turn one's head?

Luc lay spread-eagled on the floor, his throat gaping, blood pouring out in a red sheet. Eyes blind and staring. Gone.

The Fox wiped his blade against his backside and turned back to Madeleine. She didn't see him—she was pulled into a tight ball, sobbing in breathless searing gasps of pain.

RHUS TURNED BACK to the girl—and stopped.

Heavy boots pounded up the stone stairway. Curse the gods and the gods' whelps...the string of disjointed curses came out in a thick mumble, along with another strand of spit. Something wrong with his tongue. He wiped at his lips, swallowed painfully and tried to think. There was no time for the girl—the mouthy little bastard had buggered that up. Now he would have to make up some excuse for killing him, and quick.

CHAPTER NINETEEN

Turga stared moodily into the purple depths of his goblet. The wine had not lifted his black spirits; it was hard to imagine anything that would.

Bad enough that his profits leaked away with each day the auction stayed closed. It could be weeks, even months that he had to keep those children. And they had to stay healthy and strong—he couldn't just toss them into a basement dungeon and feed them scraps, not if he wanted a decent price at the end. Then that idiot Rhus had tipped the scales toward disaster by destroying a third of his merchandise. Turga could only pray he hadn't done worse.

He should never have hired the man, cousin or no. That was Turga's first mistake—letting family obligations outweigh good judgment. And they should have left Rhus behind in Baskir when he didn't promptly obey the callback. Second mistake. The man was worthless, a turd on Turga's heart.

Through the narrow window, Turga could just see the crude outbuilding tucked against the wall where Rhus was locked in isolation. There he would live or die as the Veil decreed. Better for him he should die, thought Turga, than face my justice. He hoped the ravenous worm who devoured the unworthy dead made a particularly unpleasant end to all men who knowingly spread their sickness. The thought of Rhus tramping all over his

compound with a burning head and raw throat goaded Turga
into impotent fury.

Turga had been in the midst of lambasting Rhus for the death
of the slave boy when he noticed the man was swaying on his feet.
He eyed him sharply. Was that hangdog stance and slick pallor
merely fear of the punishment to come, as Turga had assumed? As
if in reply, Rhus slowly crumpled to his knees. His throat worked
as he swallowed slowly. A string of saliva escaped his mouth and
hung in a glistening thread.

"The Hewer take you, what is wrong with you?" Turga had
taken three hasty steps backward before the words were out of
his mouth.

Rhus shrugged, armed his mouth dry and offered a brief
ghastly smile. "Guess the Veil caught up with me. Sorry, boss. I
was hoping it was just a sore throat."

Turga would have the shed torched and Rhus inside it once
he died. Maybe even if he didn't die. That was the first cheering
thought he'd had all day.

MATTHIEU NEEDED HER, she knew that. She could feel him
watching her now, knew his stricken worried eyes had hardly
strayed from her huddled form in the two days since Luc's death.
She needed to pull herself together for his sake.

But if she turned from the wall, she had nowhere to look that
wasn't a reminder of what had happened. Luc's empty cot, the
chain snaking away from its leg. Bloodstains where he had lain
with the life gushing out of him. He had kissed her, and now he
was dead. Madeleine wished she were dead as well.

"Maddy, please. You've got to eat." Matthieu's hand on her

shoulder was steady, his voice gentle and coaxing. "C'mon now. This is really good—just have a little taste." He didn't sound scared, Madeleine realized. He sounded almost like a grown-up. And something about that—her little brother taking on the job of looking after her—touched her, so that she forced herself to roll over and sit up.

Her head throbbed behind her eyes as she moved. Too much crying, or too long without food, she guessed. Though in all honesty, she didn't feel hungry.

"Thanks, Matthieu," she whispered. She took the cup he offered her and sipped. Her throat hurt too. Justine's voice came back to her then, something she had said when Madeleine was little, carrying on over some childish hurt: "Hush, now, you'll make yourself sick with crying." I guess you really can, thought Madeleine. She turned her attention to the bread her brother was holding. She didn't really want it, and it hurt to swallow it, but she ate it anyway.

She and Matthieu were family—the only family they had left. If he could be strong for her, she could do the same. She would eat and try not to think about the stain on the floor, and maybe the pain that squeezed her heart so fiercely it made her whole body ache would loosen its grip.

"Your pardon, boss."

It was Zhirak, one of very few who would venture to interrupt Turga in his current state.

"What is it?"

"Traveling peddlers at the gate—new ones. Foreigners, most of 'em. I thought you might be interested."

"Why, who are they?" Though he had a pirate's dislike of paying for his comforts, Turga had the foresight to treat fairly those within his gates. As a result, Rath Turga enjoyed a steady trickle of traffic from merchants and craftsmen hoping to increase their trade.

"Dancing girl, blacksmith—he's a jewelcrafter too, some very fine, unusual pieces. You might be able to pick them up cheap if he's yet to make his name. The girl—she's the real thing, boss, and I don't mean just beautiful. Seems like she's dancing even with her feet planted on the ground, you know? Thought she might cheer you up…"

Turga grunted. He was hardly in the mood, but moods could change. "They a pair?"

Zhirak shook his bald head. "Don't think so. But there's another guy, husband or maybe just bodyguard. Keeps a close eye on 'er and his hand to his sword."

"Right. Quite the little crew. Any more?"

"Two. The dancing girl's musician—thin dreamy type. And a remedy woman." Zhirak hesitated, and then added cautiously, "Ain't my business, boss, but I wondered if she might have any-thing for…" He finished the sentence with a vague gesture toward the window.

"No." Turga was curt but not angry. It had crossed his own mind, if not for Rhus then for any, Axe-Wielder forfend, he might turn out to have poisoned. "You know as well as I—there are a hundred different so-called remedies for the Gray Veil, and not one is worth the time it takes to tell about it. Rhus is on his own."

Still, it was an intriguing group. If he could buy up some jewelry, turn it around at a profit in Baskir, that might begin to make up for some of his recent losses. And the girl, yes, she sounded very promising indeed. But not for tonight. Tonight he wanted a sleeping draught, and he would not risk it with strangers in the compound.

"Tell them to camp outside the walls for tonight. I will see them tomorrow."

CHAPTER TWENTY

GABRIELLE WATCHED ANXIOUSLY as Yolenka made their case to the guard. Two days' dusty travel had only increased her sense of urgency. They were so close…and something was wrong, something beyond being held prisoner. She had to get to the children.

Dominic, beside her, shifted impatiently and glowered as the guard peered out at him from behind the heavy gate. It was almost more than he could endure, to stand outside politely knowing that his children were somewhere inside the clay-brick enclosure. His groan, when the guard's head abruptly withdrew and the gate thudded shut, carried to Yolenka.

"Shhh!" She frowned at him. "He gets bigger boss is all. Is stronghold here, not village market. Hard to get in. Is time now for patience."

Poor Dom, thought Gabrielle. His patience is already worn to a frazzle. Féolan must have sensed it as well, for he eased over and laid a steadying hand on Dominic's shoulder. Dominic blew out air and gave a curt nod.

Yolenka's sharp look softened. "Is hard, I know. Is good look, though, that frown. Like jealous husband." Her teasing smile lightened their mood.

"Yolenka." Derkh had kept his eyes trained on the gate. "He's back."

The man who came out to inspect them looked strong as a draft horse and only slightly smaller. His head, shaved or naturally bald, gleamed golden in the slanting rays of the sun. He examined each of them carefully as Yolenka gestured, evidently talking up their various and fantastic skills. Finally she gazed up from under her eyelids at him, flashed her teeth, raised her arms above her head and began to dance.

Only a few steps, a snatch of hummed song, a couple of languid undulations, but Gabrielle saw the effect it had. The man's interest ratcheted up immediately. More snatches of conversation, and the door was shut again.

"He ask Turga." Yolenka smiled. "We pass his main man. Is good."

MATTHIEU WATCHED HIS sister eat. He didn't need his aunt Gabrielle's skills to notice that she lacked gusto, and not just because grief and shock had taken away her appetite.

He noted how she paused before swallowing and avoided the bread crusts and the meat. He had done exactly that just last year, when he had tonsillitis. He watched for the fleeting wince as the food went down—and didn't have to wait long.

"Maddy."

Her eyes when she looked up to him were dull. Well, she'd been crying for a long time, so that might be why. But he didn't like how white her face looked.

"Does your throat hurt?"

She nodded. "And my head." She attempted a smile. "I probably just wore myself out."

Matthieu reached over and touched her forehead gingerly. It was warm and a bit damp.

"I think you have a fever."

Madeleine took another careful sip of soup and set the cup on the floor. Her fingers trembled against the side of the cup.

"Don't worry, Matthieu." She slumped back into her blanket. "I just need to sleep. I'm sure I'll be fine by morning."

He watched her for a long time, wishing Gabrielle were there, wishing he knew what to do. Wondering if there was anyone in the fortress who would help, and if he could even make them understand what was needed. I'll wait until tomorrow, he thought. If Maddy's any worse tomorrow, I'll holler and try to make them help her.

YOLENKA WAS UNPERTURBED at being shut out for the night. Dominic, frantic for his children and unused to taking orders, was livid.

Derkh, who had said very little since Rath Turga had loomed into sight, spoke up now.

"This is what it's like all over Greffier. You don't enter towns at night. You don't see important people without going through channels. This guy is a warlord—he has a lot of enemies; he has to be careful. Honestly, Dominic, I think if we get in tomorrow, we're doing pretty well."

"What are we supposed to do then—just sit here and mumble our tongues?" Dominic's hand clenched again around the hilt of his sword.

"You are joking, yes?" Yolenka was already halfway inside the wagon, rummaging in the storage bins. She grunted as she hauled out Derkh's anvil and let it thud to the ground. She unhooked the portable brazier hanging on the outside of the wagon and flipped down the horizontal wooden shutter at the back and propped it up with a board to make a little table.

She straightened and swept her eyes around the little group like a general about to address his troops.

"We are open for business."

Gabrielle stared at her. They all did. Yolenka didn't actually expect her to peddle remedies and charms when her niece and nephew were in who knew what straits?

Yolenka huffed and flapped her hands at them. "Is work time! You think I am not real? We do good trade tonight, or Turga will know it."

She clambered over the propped shutter and into the wagon. Untying the canvas curtain, she addressed them once more. "I put on costume. Derkh starts up fire. Then we set up remedies on table here. You—she pointed at Féolan—start playing, let people know we are here."

The curtain flapped shut.

DERKH HAMMERED THE last ring closed, doused it in his bucket and gave all the fittings a final check before handing the ox-yoke back to the silent farmer who stood waiting beside him. Yolenka, dazzling in her bright silks and paint, had already negotiated the price of Derkh's repair and insisted on payment in advance.

She was tireless, everywhere at once: translating, haggling, changing money. Whenever a cluster of men appeared at their camp through the fortress gates or from the surrounding countryside, she summoned Féolan to play and mesmerized them with the sultry undulating dance that made Derkh feel as though the coals in his smith's brazier had fanned into sudden flame deep within his own body. He hated that she did this for strangers, hated to see his own feelings mirrored in their rough faces. But she only laughed as she collected their coins and tucked them provocatively into her waist or between her breasts. She bent down to whisper in Derkh's ear as she passed. "This is just fool playing. I save real dancing for boss-man, tomorrow."

For me! Derkh wanted to shout. Save the real dancing for me! But he said nothing, bent his arm to his task and brought his mind back to their purpose. His feelings for Yolenka would have to wait.

Amazing, it was, how customers had appeared out of nowhere once they had set up shop. Word must have spread that day as they traveled through villages and farms, the people just waiting for them to set down. Their first visitor had slipped from within the gates of Rath Turga minutes after Féolan began to play—not the rough pirate Derkh had expected, but a worried mother with a coughing child. Gabrielle had had a steady trickle of patients ever since. Derkh hoped she wouldn't have any serious cases—he knew how hard she would find it to turn anyone away, but they couldn't afford to let her exhaust herself now. That thought had barely been formed when his memory protested: She exhausted herself for you, when you were an enemy soldier. Derkh snorted, impatient with his own thoughts, and turned to the leaky bucket his next customer presented. Just as well I'm a tradesman, not a judge, he thought.

And so the strange night passed, all of them busy except for Dominic, who was relegated to security and smith's helper. The poor guy, Derkh thought, watching him pace the perimeter of their little camp yet again. He had never seen a man more in need of action.

CHAPTER TWENTY-ONE

TURGA SLEPT LATE AND TOOK HIS TIME with his food and his toilet. He was much restored, the gloom of the previous night dispelled by his usual alert confidence. By early afternoon, when he called for an audience with the peddlers, he was ready to relish both profitable trade and a beautiful woman.

Zhirak had not exaggerated about the woman. She was glorious, pacing into his chamber like a tawny panther.

The others paled by comparison, but still he observed them closely as they were introduced. The husband seemed rather on edge—one would be, he supposed, married to a woman who made men pant over her like dogs for a living. He didn't envy the fellow his role. It was the musician who caught his eye—Zhirak's description had not prepared him for the man's unusual presence. *Brightness*, you could almost call it. Burning with an artist's vision, no doubt, Turga thought with dry amusement. Well, he wasn't here to admire pretty eyes, not on a man at least.

"I'm told you are a fine dancer," he said. To his surprise, the woman who had introduced herself as Yolenka laughed scornfully.

"Your men said that?" Her golden eyes flashed at him from under dark eyelashes, teasing and intimate. Like he was an old friend, not a feared warlord. Her voice lowered.

"I gave them garbage—dance you can see in any cheap tavern. Just a sniff from the wine bottle, yes?"

She had come closer to him as she spoke, floated maybe for he hadn't noticed her take a step. He could smell the scent on her hair, see the black paint that accentuated the line of her eyes. She flashed white teeth at him.

"The wine I saved for you. I wanted to offer you a personal performance—just you in the audience, or you and your invited guests. Both, if you like. Your choice, of course."

As though just noticing her own forwardness, Yolenka offered an apologetic smile and returned to the others—giving him the opportunity to watch her shoulders and hips as she glided away. Mother of all, she was good. Her every breath was a performance. She spoke over her shoulder as she took her place with the others.

"It's not home brew I offer. I was first dancer with Riko's troupe. Perhaps you have heard of him?"

Turga had heard—he had seen the troupe perform. The dancers had been stunning, all of them.

He narrowed his eyes, suspicious of this new claim.

"Why did you leave?"

Yolenka shrugged, a languid ripple that was worlds away from any man's version of the same gesture.

"I hurt my knee touring in the north of the Krylian lands. That's where I met this lot. So I'll admit right now—I can't do a series of backflips and land on one leg. But,"—and again the eyes and teeth flashed at him—"everything else works just fine, I promise you."

That business was soon concluded. Turga didn't even haggle

much over the price, or demand that she end her performance in his bed. Like all Tarzines, he held true artistry in high respect.

FÉOLAN FOUND IT HARD to follow Turga's unfamiliar voice, but he was able to understand much of Yolenka's end of the negotiation. He too saw the skill in her performance, but he also felt a twinge on Derkh's behalf. He hoped he wouldn't be asked to translate.

When they moved on to Derkh's jewelry, however, Yolenka became all business. Turga noticed this with, Féolan thought, amused respect. Yolenka had kept the jewelry under wraps the night before, wanting to offer Turga the chance of an exclusive purchase. "Also, you don't have so much," she pointed out. "We save until we get inside." Turga clearly liked the pieces, though Féolan gathered he was disappointed there weren't more in gold. Rather heated negotiations followed, before Yolenka announced that Turga had commissioned gold ear pendants and bracelets like the ones Derkh was displaying in silver, as well as two neckplates in the same style as hers, and that she had agreed on condition that he purchase their entire existing stock.

"Yolenka," Derkh protested, "I can't—" And was cut off with a hissed admonition: "You are trader. Traders always have time to fill rich orders." Derkh gulped and nodded meekly.

More followed—talk of lodging, meals, free passage to offer trade outside the walls or shipside. Soon they were unloading their clothes from the caravan into a large communal room beside the scullery at the back of the fortress and setting Derkh and Gabrielle up for business in its treeless courtyard.

"Is too hot here," Yolenka proclaimed. "Patients will burn

in Derkh's fire. I go ask for"—she waved vaguely above her head
to indicate shade—"tent thing."

THE AWNING HELPED, Derkh had to admit. So did the two
proper workbenches—one for his jewelry work, the other to
display swords and knives—that Yolenka managed to scare up.
Gabrielle's remedies were once again displayed on the little shelf,
with the emptied caravan serving as clinic. If this were really
their business, they'd be in pretty good shape.

Yolenka had more than done her part. Now it was up to
them to find the children and get them away. Derkh had no idea
where to start—and would have little chance to think about it
between Turga's order and the repairs that were already coming
in. His role, it seemed, would be to act busy and provide a screen
for the real players. Dominic and Féolan were slumped in the
scant shade of the outer wall, deep in talk.

Not knowing what else to do, Derkh added fuel to his little
forge and worked the bellows vigorously. A portable brazier took
constant tending to reach a temperature high enough to turn an
iron rod first red, then white-hot. He thrust one now into the
fire's incandescent heart and turned to his next task.

"So—WHAT HAVE we learned?"

It was late, past midnight, before they were able to gather
together in their room. Dominic, cross-legged on his mattress
and intent, nodded at Derkh to start.

Precious little, it seemed. Derkh had learned that the Tarzine
pirates would pay handsomely for Basin-style swords and knives.
It was a good thing he had stowed away enough weapons to keep

their own party well outfitted. Gabrielle learned which men wanted love charms and which had foot ulcers, but Yolenka's bright chatter with the various customers had failed to turn up any rumor of the captive children.

Dominic had gone to check on their mule—an excuse for getting inside the stables. There were only about a dozen horses, he reported. "It doesn't seem much for all the men here."

"Turga's ships are his horses," Yolenka reminded them.

"Anyway, if we do manage to find the children, steal some horses and get away, there won't be many left to chase us on," Dominic concluded glumly. "Féolan, I assume if you had found them we'd know?"

Féolan nodded. He had managed to explore a fair bit of the fortress unobserved and had found more than one passageway kept off-limits by a guard, but had not been able to discover whether those halls led to Turga's private chambers, the women's quarters, a treasury—or a jail block.

"I did discover one odd thing," he said. "There's a man locked in one of the outbuildings. You know that jumble of sheds against the wall—they are pretty much all locked, but I was knocking on the walls, thinking if the children were inside they would answer. And when this fellow yelled back to me, Great Mother, I was sure I had found them. But it was only the one Tarzine man."

And they had all learned that Yolenka was, indeed, a glorious dancer. She had performed that evening in the courtyard with the entire fortress in attendance, and it was lucky she had warned them to act "bored" with the show because they had all been transfixed. They had already seen how seductive she could be, but even Féolan had not been prepared for what she could do with room to move. The following evening was to be a private performance for Turga alone, and she had promised him "even better."

None of which got them any closer to a rescue.

CHAPTER TWENTY-TWO

MADELEINE SEEMED A LITTLE BETTER the next morning. She'd had a proper sleep, her first since Luc's death, and she looked herself again. The sore throat was worse, though—that was obvious even before breakfast, as soon as she took her first sip of water. Matthieu couldn't tell if she really felt better, or if she was just trying harder.

"I don't feel too bad, really," she insisted. Matthieu looked pointedly at the remains of her breakfast. She had left everything that wasn't either liquid or mushy. "Apart from my throat, I mean," Madeleine said. "It's really sore. But I'm not horribly feverish or achy. I don't think it's anything very serious."

By lunchtime, Matthieu wasn't so sure. Madeleine was back in bed, headachy and weak. She didn't even try to eat.

It was time to start hollering.

YOLENKA HAD LEFT Gabrielle and Derkh to their work, leaving Féolan as halting translator, to investigate the guardhouse by the gate.

"I wish I could get in there," Dominic had said that morning. "How many guards are on duty at a time? What kind of alarm do they have?"

Yolenka had grinned, and slowly, teasingly, pulled an intricately carved little box from some hidden pocket in her skirts. It rattled as she shook it.

"Leave this to me."

"What is that?" Dominic spoke for them all.

"Is *reneñas*." The grin became broader. "I have not met a soldier who can resist a game…or who can win over me."

So in the sleepy heat of midafternoon, when Gabrielle's trickle of patients had dried up to nothing and Derkh had pulled out his jeweler's tools to begin roughing out Turga's order, Yolenka ambled off to play *reneñas* with the guards.

With no patients, without Yolenka to give them the illusion of purpose, the futility of their charade crept over Gabrielle like some waking version of the gray fog of her dream. It was pointless, this busy hammering and dancing and doling out of tonics. Urgency drummed within her, goading her to hurry—if only she knew where.

Someone was hurrying. She looked up as footsteps rapped across the baked clay of the courtyard and was surprised to see Turga himself striding toward them. He did not look happy.

"Derkh. Get Yolenka. Hurry!" Féolan could speak enough Tarzine to stumble through a simple pick-up or payment, but not this. Whatever "this" was.

Turga's tawny skin flushed dark with annoyance as Féolan tried to explain Yolenka's absence. Finally she came hurrying from the gatehouse and took her place at Gabrielle's side. Turga fired out a question.

Yolenka faltered. Turga snapped his fingers at her, impatient with the delay. Slowly, she turned to Gabrielle.

"He ask…he ask if you are afraid to treat the Gray Veil."

"The Gray Veil? What is that?" Whatever was rampaging through Baskir, was her first guess.

Yolenka swallowed, her eyes worried. "Is very bad sickness, makes sick person strangle in the throat. It spreads fast, can kill anybody but"—and her voice went very quiet now—"always more children die."

FÉOLAN WATCHED GABRIELLE'S color drain to ashy gray, longed to jump up and comfort her and steeled himself not to. He remembered her dream, her constant anxiety in recent days about the children, and knew her fear. She'll give us away to Turga, he worried, and then saw in the man's grim dismissal that he interpreted her reaction as fear of the disease itself. Looks like he expected as much, Féolan thought. He gathered his strength and sent it out to Gabrielle.

She was already pulling herself together. He saw it in the straightening of her back. Felt it as his mind touched hers.

"Ask him who is sick, Yolenka. Ask like you are curious, not worried."

The reply confirmed their fears. Yolenka could not keep the emotion from her voice as she passed on Turga's words.

"Is girl. He say she is just slave, but worth good price." She hesitated, glancing at Dominic, but he gestured at her to go on. His face was wooden with the effort to hide his feelings.

"He say he does not want lose his profit."

GABRIELLE FOLLOWED ZHIRAK up the narrow stone stairway, wondering how on earth she would stop the children from giving her away. Turga's instructions—to stand in the doorway as far from "the girl" as possible and attempt to diagnose her illness from there—worried her too. It went against her instincts to keep a distance from any patient—let alone her own niece.

The landing was close now, and no telling how nearby the children were kept. Could she call out to them? She had not yet encountered anyone who spoke Krylaise, but still, her actions might seem suspicious.

A tune popped into her head—a little children's nonsense song that she had sung to the kids when they were little. Was bursting into song on the way to diagnose a terrifying disease any less suspicious than shouting out a warning? Maybe not—but she was running out of time. She took a breath and began to sing, first under her breath as if to herself and then loudly, as the words fell into place:

"Madeleine, just keep silent
Matthieu, please be quiet
Pretend you don't know me
And safe you will be.

"Madeleine, just keep silent
Matthieu, please be quiet
Pretend you don't know me
And safe you will be."

They met a guard at the top of the stairs, who pulled out a ring of keys, led her to the third door and opened it. He stood back, unwilling it seemed to enter the room himself.

Gabrielle took a deep steadying breath and stepped inside.

Matthieu sat on a cot, his shorn head in his hands. His body was rigid with effort as he stared at the floor. She heard him sniff, understood he was fighting tears as well as the need to fling himself against her. Her own tears, pity and anger and relief combined, welled hot in her eyes, and she was glad the guard could not see.

"Hi," she said softly, striving for the neutral, calming tone she used so often in her work as a healer. "Don't say anything yet. Don't even look until you feel ready." The room was dim and too warm, but Matthieu seemed all right. Madeleine, she saw, lay on a cot on the far side of the room, apparently asleep.

"My dad—" The words came out in a rush of breath.

"He's here," said Gabrielle. The narrow shoulders straightened, and she felt Matthieu's wave of exultation, but he kept his face down. She pitched her voice lower. "We are going to get you home, but you have to be patient. We're still figuring things out. Right now, they sent me to look at your sister. How is she?"

Now, slowly, Matthieu lowered his hands and turned toward her. His brown eyes, shining with tears and hope and worry, squeezed at her heart. She wanted nothing more than to rush over and gather him into her arms—but she couldn't.

"Matthieu, I'm not allowed to come in—not yet. I have to report back to Turga, and then I hope he'll send me to heal Madeleine. But I need to try to figure out what's wrong with her."

Matthieu nodded. His eyes darted to a third cot, an empty one, and away. There was a rusty patch on the floor nearby. Gabrielle had seen stains like that before. What had happened here?

"At first I thought she was just sad," Matthieu said. "We had—" He swallowed, tried again. "There was another boy here. He was killed and…" Matthieu was crying openly now, and Gabrielle found herself on the cot beside him, holding him tight, Turga's rule forgotten. She would do no less for any strange child.

A heavy tread, a startled exclamation. They both looked up to see the guard's head in the doorway. His barked command and gesture were plain enough. Gabrielle settled for one last squeeze and reluctantly returned to her station in the doorway.

Slowly, Matthieu found his voice. "Maddy wouldn't eat or talk or do anything for a couple of days, she was so upset. But then yesterday, I got her to sit up and eat. That's when I realized she was sick too."

"How does she feel, Matthieu?"

"Mostly she has a really sore throat. A bit of fever and headache too, I think, but not too bad. She doesn't seem all that sick, but she's been sleeping most of the day." He looked up at Gabrielle. "Her voice sounds funny."

"Funny how?" Gabrielle kept her tone level, but Matthieu's words had given her a chill. Yolenka had had only a moment to describe the progression of the Gray Veil to her, but Madeleine's symptoms fit. On the other hand, they fit any number of common childhood illnesses. She clung to that thought.

"I dunno. Kind of like she's talking through her nose. It just sounds different from normal."

"Okay, that's a good observation." Gabrielle smiled at Matthieu. "You'd make a good bonemender."

That won a smile, though fleeting. "What are you going to do now?" he asked.

Gabrielle considered. "I don't think I'm going to wake her up. If I can't examine her, I doubt I can learn much more from her than you just told me, and it will be hard for her to pretend like you did."

Matthieu nodded. "Can I tell her when she wakes up?"

"You'd better!" Gabrielle smiled again. "And I think I will be back soon. Right now I'm just going to see if I can sense anything more."

Gabrielle closed her eyes, let the world fade away and stretched out her mind to the sleeping girl. Madeleine's sleep was uneasy—Gabrielle could feel her discomfort, the occasional flares of pain that must come from her throat. She did not get the feeling of desperate illness—Matthieu was right in that. But there was something else, wasn't there? Like a fungus growing secretly in the dark, some vague sense of looming threat.

Gabrielle didn't know if Madeleine had caught the Gray Veil. But her niece was in danger.

That Gabrielle knew beyond doubt.

CHAPTER TWENTY-THREE

*Z*HIRAK KEPT A GOODLY DISTANCE between them as he escorted her back to Turga, Gabrielle noticed. And Turga himself was so far away she practically had to shout. He was seated against the wall of his audience chamber and held a hand up to stop her as soon as she was in the door.

"Does it really spread that easily?" she asked Yolenka who was stationed at Turga's side.

"He is more careful than most." Gabrielle had never seen Yolenka so subdued. She lifted worried amber eyes to Gabrielle. "I will not say he is stupid."

Turga barked out a question.

"Does she have it?"

"I can't tell for sure without examining her," Gabrielle replied. "I have seen children with similar symptoms who had nothing but a bad cold. But—"

He interrupted abruptly.

"Does she have sore throat?"

"Yes." There was no reason to sugarcoat it. If Turga believed Madeleine had the Veil, he would send Gabrielle back to treat her.

Turga's features tightened. There followed a long exchange with Yolenka.

"He say, if you treat, you stay in cell until she is better and you and boy are for sure also healthy. If she die, you leave Rath Turga, not touch anything or go near any person. He pay two bars of gold if both live. He say nothing if girl dies, but I say he must pay for your danger. He say half bar of gold then."

Gabrielle understood the need for such bargaining, but it shocked her all the same. She tried to collect her wits.

"All right, of course. No, wait—Yolenka, tell him I will do it if the others in the group agree. I need to talk with them first."

"TONIGHT? BUT HOW will you get the children past the guards? Or avoid pursuit?"

"We have between now and midnight to figure that out." Dominic was grim with determination, but Gabrielle knew he was no closer to an answer than she was. "If we don't come up with a plan, we'll have to postpone it," he admitted. "But assume that once Yolenka's performance is finished, we will come for you."

Gabrielle had told them all she could—the location of the room, the position of the guards, the little she could offer about the type of lock on the door. She had brewed up whatever medicines she had that might be of help and learned everything Yolenka could tell her about the Gray Veil. It was time.

THE GUARD RETREATED to the end of the hall as quickly as he could, and Gabrielle did not hold back. She swept Matthieu into her arms and held him tight. For once, he didn't wiggle away impatiently. Gabrielle could feel the tumult of warring emotions within him, realized that if she held him much longer he would give way to the sobs he was trying with all his might to overcome. She eased back, and Matthieu followed her lead.

"I think you should see Maddy right away. She seems a lot worse."

The worry in his voice was enough to take her at once to her niece's bedside.

Madeleine was awake, watching them. She mustered a wan smile for Gabrielle, and then the tears came, welling up and spilling down her cheeks. She didn't seem to have the energy to wipe them away.

Gabrielle smoothed the tangled hair away from the girl's face and gently wiped the wet streaks off her cheeks.

"Hello, dear one," she murmured. "It's okay now, Maddy, we're going to look after you. We're going to get you better and take you home."

Madeleine did look worse. Her fever was only a little higher, but the blue eyes were dull and her skin shone with sweat.

"Is your throat still sore?" asked Gabrielle.

Madeleine nodded slowly as if it pained her.

"Really sore." The words came out nasal and slightly slurred, each syllable an effort. A thin track of spittle spilled from the corner of her mouth.

"Can I take a look?"

The foul odor of Madeleine's breath almost made Gabrielle recoil. She knew, of course, that a throat infection sours the breath, but she had never smelled anything so awful on a child. Her belly tightened. Yolenka had described exactly this.

The room was too dim, however, to see into a person's mouth.

And it was late—it would only get darker from now on. Gabrielle looked around the little cell. There was one patch of strong light on the floor, streaming in through the high narrow window.

"Matthieu, I need to get Madeleine into that bright spot. Can you help me?"

Was she endangering Matthieu, getting him so close to his sister? Gabrielle hesitated. Surely he had already been exposed.

Matthieu was at her side instantly.

"C'mon Maddy, out of bed with you!"

Madeleine's lips twitched into a smile, and Gabrielle marveled at Matthieu's deft touch. He's like Tristan, she thought, so carefree and silly, but when you need him, he doesn't hold back.

Between them, they helped Madeleine slip out of bed and lie down on the floor, her head angled into the sunlight. Now Gabrielle could get a good look.

And there it was—the gray plaque growing over Madeleine's tonsils. The Gray Veil. Mottled, leathery and alien, it lay over the girl's throat like some parasitic leech. It's just an illness, like any other, Gabrielle told herself—but she could not shake the revulsion she felt at the sight of that gray coating.

She got Madeleine tucked back into bed and coaxed the willowbark tea into her, spoonful by spoonful, encouraging her through each reluctant swallow. Then she settled herself beside the little cot, took one hot trembly hand in hers and closed her eyes.

"It's just the one guard, but we'll have to take care of him before he raises an alarm."

Féolan and Derkh both nodded in agreement. They were not permitted to bring weapons into the stronghold, but Féolan's thin blade could be strapped against the inside of a man's thigh where it easily escaped the casual inspection given to wandering peddlers. Derkh had managed a decent copy of the cunning Elvish work, so they had two between them.

"The guard has a key to the cell," continued Dominic, "but we aren't sure about Madeleine's manacle." Surely the gods would not send him such a fate, he prayed—to have to choose between leaving one child or losing both.

"If I can smuggle in Derkh's filigree tool, I'm pretty sure I can pick that lock," offered Féolan.

"You'll have to get away right after Yolenka's dance then," said Dominic. "We'll be waiting for you."

"Getting in isn't the problem, though, is it?" Derkh didn't like to state the obvious, but without a viable escape plan there was no rescue. "We could fight our way out of the building, even with the kids, but then there are the three guards at the gate…"

"And the ten horses in the stable. I know."

They had spun all kinds of wild scenarios—somehow killing both the fortress and gatehouse guards without raising an alarm, overwhelming the stable hands and leaving half a dozen horses saddled and ready to fly from the stronghold, even sneaking in and killing the horses (which would not prevent Turga's men from *running* after them, with every chance of quickly catching up). Nothing had promised any real chance of success.

Dominic dropped his head into his hands and screwed his eyes shut. There had to be a way. But in the darkness came another terrible thought: Even if he got the children safely back to the ship, would they live? Whatever this Gray Veil was, it was enough to make Yolenka, who appeared cowed by nothing, subdued and tense. And Turga, by all accounts, lived in fear of the very words.

Before he could thrust it away, his fear took shape behind his eyelids: He saw his two children—his babies!—lifeless on the deck, shrouded in saffron sailcloth, two unbearably sad silent bundles. The terror that clutched his belly at the sight made him groan aloud.

He opened his eyes, tried to blink the vision away, but the image was stuck now in his brain. Two bundles, two limp and lifeless—

Dominic straightened, his face caught in comical transition from despair to excitement.

"We'll say they're dead."

Twin blank confused looks greeted his announcement. He held up a hand, stalling their questions, thinking it through.

"I'm serious. We'll say the children are dead. We'll bundle them up like corpses and carry them out. People here, they're afraid to get within ten feet of this disease. We'll say…" Dominic groped after something that made sense. "We'll say it was part of Turga's deal with Gabrielle—that if they died, we would get them out of here before anyone else could catch it."

The two men were nodding now, seeing the possibilities.

"If Turga shows up, we're in trouble," said Féolan. "And we'll have to hope no one gets curious about how Matthieu went so quickly. But I think you're right, Dom—they won't want to get close enough to investigate, they'll just be glad to see the end of us."

CHAPTER TWENTY-FOUR

URGA LOUNGED BACK on his mound of sumptuous silk-covered cushions, a picture of elegant detachment. Or so he hoped. He admired and enjoyed a stirring performance, but was not about to show this fallen dance-mistress just how unsettling and exciting she was.

He thought he had seen her best when she cut loose in the open courtyard. There, the sensuous promise of what she had called the "sniff from the wine bottle" had been married to a breath-taking athleticism that proved her boasts about her past career. Now, though, in his private quarters, she revealed yet another side: provocative, lyrical, intimate. As though all the moods and passions of a lover were turned into dance, he thought.

The musician, on the other hand, was barely adequate. Turga had the distinct impression that the poor fellow was struggling to keep up with Yolenka. At times it seemed the dance was entirely new to him, that he was learning it as he went along.

Perhaps it was so. Yolenka had promised Turga something just for him. Was she inventing this dance on the spot, tailoring it to how she judged his taste? If so, she was a discerning woman indeed.

Too soon the performance drew to a close, and Yolenka kneeled before him in the classical dancer's courtesy, the bright, fluttering veils and sashes pooling around her.

It was irresistible. He threw detachment to the winds and stood, clapping loud and long. Yolenka tossed her mane back from her face. Her golden eyes caught his as she offered a slow smile of acknowledgment. A sheen of sweat gleamed on her forehead and across her collarbones. Turga pictured himself drying it off with jasmine-scented toweling. Then he pictured himself kissing it off, and a bolt of desire ran through him. What he could do with a woman like this!

But though Turga cared little for law, his personal scruples were ironclad. He would not pressure an artist of her caliber. He offered a hand and raised Yolenka to her feet, turned and poured two generous glasses of wine and held one out.

"Magnificent. It was everything you promised and more. Riko must have been very upset at losing you." He placed the glass into her hand and waggled the other at the musician seated against the wall. "Here, tell him he is welcome. Though I must say his talent is not a match to your own."

Yolenka grinned and winked. "I threw him a few surprises tonight. He does well enough when he is better rehearsed."

She tossed back half the wine, glided over until she was almost—but not quite—touching Turga and looked up at him through her eyelashes. "I thought I might surprise him again, and send him back without me," she whispered. "I thought we might like to be better acquainted."

"We might indeed," Turga agreed. "Perhaps he would like to take his wine with him."

Another blinding private smile, and Yolenka was pacing across the room to—what was the man's name? Faylor, Faylon, something like that.

Turga watched the exchange that followed with amused interest. The musician was not happy—that much was clear. He argued with Yolenka, quietly at first and then more heatedly. She tossed her head and spoke sharply. The man spread out his arms in protest or supplication, but Yolenka brushed him off like a serving boy and turned her back on him.

"He's worried about your man, no doubt," offered Turga. "Aren't you?"

"Who, Dominic?" She gave a snort of laughter. "Dom will be deep in his own goblet by now. If by some unlikely chance he isn't, Féolan will see to it. My husband won't know if I return at moonrise or sunrise."

Turga chuckled in approval and slipped an arm around Yolenka's waist.

The musician gave her one last despairing look. She flapped her hand at him, shooing him off.

And they were alone.

RELUCTANTLY, GABRIELLE PULLED herself away from the silent unseen battle raging in Madeleine's throat and eased her awareness back into the world. If Dominic did come, she needed to be alert. It wouldn't do to be caught in a dazed half-trance.

She didn't like to leave Madeleine, though. The infection had spread, and it was strong. It had taken Gabrielle all this time just to build a ring of protective light around the edges of the darkened patches that marked the boundaries of its encroachment and to push it back the tiniest bit.

And even then, even with the infection contained, Gabrielle could feel Madeleine growing weaker. Some other force was at work that Gabrielle did not understand. The girl's pulse had become rapid and faint, and she was very pale.

Perhaps she should keep working. There was a good chance Dom would not attempt the rescue tonight anyway.

"Matthieu," she said, "keep your ears open. If you hear anything unusual at all—even just footsteps on the stairs—you wake me up right away, all right?"

She could just see Matthieu's nod in the scanty candlelight. "Is my dad coming?"

"It's possible," said Gabrielle. "The time may not be right. But if the plan falls into place, we are going to get you out tonight."

She did not add that, to her knowledge, there was no actual plan.

"GODS OF THE DEEP, what kept you?" Dominic had been pacing the confines of their room since nightfall. No bells or horns marked the passage of time here, but it seemed to Dominic that Yolenka could have performed three dances since she and Féolan had left for Turga's chambers.

Dominic peered behind Féolan. "Where's Yolenka?"

Féolan's mouth tightened. "Both questions have the same answer, but it had better wait. We should get moving."

They made their way through the fortress, not sneaking exactly but doing their best to avoid notice. Féolan filled Dominic in under this breath.

"I cannot guess what she is up to," he concluded.

"You don't suppose she means to betray us?" asked Dominic. It was his first alarmed thought, but he could not believe it of her. Not after all she had done to help them.

Féolan shook his head. "She will not give us away, I am sure of it. Perhaps she means to deflect Turga's attention."

They paused in the shadow of a hallway while two servants bustled past with jugs of wine and a platter of food. Then Féolan continued.

"Dominic—she said if she wasn't back in time, we should leave without her."

Dominic did not reply. They were close now to the stairway Gabrielle had described, and his thoughts were all on his children and the task at hand.

"That's it?" He nodded to the shadowed stairwell at the far end of the hall.

Féolan nodded. "You sure you don't want me to go up first?"

Only Féolan was light-footed enough to creep up the stairs and take the guard by surprise. But it sat ill with Dominic to send another to do his work, especially work as unpleasant as this. He shook his head.

"No—let's stick to the plan."

And they started up the stairs, making no attempt to hide their footfalls.

The guard who met them at the top did not seem overly alarmed. He laid his sword across the doorway to bar their way and spoke to them amiably enough in Tarzine. Féolan replied with the words he had practiced.

"We need to speak to the remedy woman."

The man shook his head emphatically. Dominic couldn't follow what he said, but his gestures were clear enough—he pointed behind him, presumably to the room where the children were being held and clutched at his neck and pointed into his open mouth.

Féolan nodded patiently and spoke more words in halting Tarzine. Dominic heard the name "Turga." Silently he eased back his coat and wrapped his hand around the knife hasp. If the man didn't buy their story, they would have to overpower him.

The guard stared at Féolan for a long moment and stepped back slowly. He walked them a few steps down the dark hallway and gestured toward a door. He was not about to go closer.

The two men made as if to walk on past the guard. Dom steeled himself as he drew up level to the man. He had never killed in cold deliberation before. He hoped to all the gods he wouldn't have to this time. But if the technique Gabrielle had suggested didn't work, and fast, he would have no other choice. His left arm snaked out around the guard's neck and wrenched the man backward off his feet. His right hand pressed his opponent's head forward while his left arm squeezed. Pray heaven he was pressing on the right spots, he thought, as the man thrashed and kicked…and then slumped against him. Amazing. Who would have thought a bonemender would know such things?

"Count a slow five once he passes out," Gabrielle had said. "Much more, and you risk killing him. You're cutting off the heart paths that send blood to his brain."

Dominic gave it six-and-a-half. That wasn't "much" more, and they could not afford for this fellow to recover his wits too soon. Féolan was ready with a gag and rope. Trussed securely, with his mouth stuffed like a goose, the guard would be unable to raise much of an alarm.

It was the work of a moment to unclip the key ring from the

guard's belt, and an agonizing age before he found the right key and was inside at last. And then Matthieu was pressed against him and Dominic bent down and lifted him high into his arms like he had when Matthieu was a little boy, held him tight and close while Matthieu wrapped his legs around his waist and wept into his neck.

"I knew you'd come for us. I told Maddy you'd find a way. I knew it."

CHAPTER TWENTY-FIVE

B Y THE TIME DOMINIC was able to pull his attention away from his son, Féolan had dragged the guard into the far corner of the cell and was working on the manacle clamped around Madeleine's ankle. The delicate skin there was chafed raw, and the sight affected Dominic more deeply than anything so far. With a low cry of anger, he started toward the end of her bed.

Gabrielle's hand on his shoulder restrained him.

"Dom."

He turned, his anger jumping like lightning from the pirates to his sister. Just for a moment. Her serious sympathetic face cooled him instantly.

"That's the least of Madeleine's problems right now. We need to get her to safety, where I can help her."

Dominic's eyes went to his daughter's face. He had thought her asleep, but saw now it wasn't so. She was watching him, not with the round, bright eyes he was used to but through half-opened heavy lids. He sank to his knees beside her.

"Sweetheart."

A ghost of a smile. "Dada." Her baby name for him, whispered on a puff of foul breath.

She was very sick, Dominic realized, worse than Gabrielle had reported that afternoon. How had she sunk so low with his

sister by her side? He had thought Gabrielle could heal anything, but even her mysterious powers must have their limits.
A knife-twist of fear stabbed his belly.

"Hah!" Dominic hadn't heard the click that signaled Féolan's
success, but he heard the Elf's satisfied sigh and the clank of the
manacle hitting the ground. Madeleine was free.

They must go. Dominic pulled his wits together and
explained their plan.

"Matthieu, can you do it?" he concluded. "It could be hard,
if there's a delay or we get questioned. You must stay still and
silent, even if it's hot or itchy or…"

Matthieu cut him off. "I know what to do," he said, "and
I'm used to being hot and itchy. Let's get away from here."

Féolan and Gabrielle had already spread out the first
blanket. Without another word, Matthieu lay down in the
middle and folded his arms. Féolan bent to wrap him up.

"Wait," said Matthieu. "That's not how they do it here."
How did he know, wondered Dominic, but both the press of
time and Matthieu's suddenly closed face kept him from asking.
He watched as his son flipped over to his stomach diagonal
on the blanket, and directed Féolan to fold over first the head
and foot, then the sides of the blanket. "Now turn me over
and tie the sides in front, over my stomach," his muffled voice
instructed.

It chilled Dominic to see his son shrouded like a corpse.
Tempting fate, the country folk would call it. But necessity
trumped superstition, and he bent to the rough bundle and
hoisted it into his arms.

"Okay in there, Matthieu?"

Féolan had offered to carry Madeleine. "I do not have Gabrielle's power, but I can lend her some strength or soothe her if she is restless."

If she is restless we are lost, thought Dominic. And if Yolenka is not waiting for us, ready to talk them past the guards...What then?

ANY MINUTE SOMEONE would wonder why he was standing by the caravan with the mule in the middle of the night. Derkh had long since done as much as he could to ready things without being obvious. The spare swords were unpacked and handy; their essential belongings were stowed. The mule's harness was laid out on the floor of the wagon. The forge and anvil he left set up outside, as if ready for use the next day. He had gone for the mule before nightfall, returning a piece of tack he had repaired that day, ambling to the mule's stall, giving her an apple and a grooming, and leading her out as if (he hoped) he was just giving her some air and exercise. After a nominal walk about the grounds, he tethered her by the caravan.

There he waited, trying to act as if he had some business out there. The night grew dark and cool—a relief to Derkh's hot skin, which was red and taut from the constant sun. The moon rose. Surely Yolenka's dance was well over by now. The night crept on. The grounds were empty now but for the odd straggler heading late to his bed.

Derkh's alert readiness was slowly replaced by alarm. They should be here by now. If something went wrong in the fortress, how would he know? Maybe they needed help, and he should go in.

He was halfway across the grounds when the doors opened and he saw them. They were walking, not running, and no guards followed or yelled after them. It had worked out, then.

Derkh checked his impulse to run to meet them. He shouldn't look like he was expecting them. He waited—and as they made their way across the dusty yard to him he noticed something. His belly did a slow clench.

"Okay, you can hitch up the mule," said Dominic as he drew near. "We'll lay the children down in the caravan."

But Derkh stood motionless, caught up in his own fore-boding.

"Where's Yolenka?"

ALL WAS IN READINESS, and still Yolenka had not come. Each passing moment increased the chance that Turga would hear of their leaving or the jailed guard be discovered.

Dominic took Féolan aside and spoke low in his ear.

"Can you do this, Féolan, without her?"

They had done nothing but motion to the bundled bodies at the door of the fortress and the guards had waved them through in hasty alarm. They knew who Gabrielle was and what she was doing in that upper room.

The gatehouse would be different. Who came and went through Turga's outer walls was closely watched.

Féolan was already trying to put together the Tarzine words in his mind. He thought back through the conversations he had overheard, especially those between Yolenka and Turga. Had they never used the word "death" or "dead"?

Something tugged at the edge of memory. Gabrielle had

pulled a long festering piece of decking from a sailor's foot. The pirate had said something, laughing harshly, to Yolenka, words that had meant little to Féolan at the time. Now the meaning came clear: "Thought I was like to die from a damn splinter."

"I'll do my best, Dominic," he replied. He didn't bother to add the obvious: that Yolenka would do it much better. Instead he glanced back to where Derkh stood, his eyes trained on the fortress.

"I'll tell Derkh."

DERKH HAD KNOWN in his bones they would be leaving without her from the moment he realized she had not come out with the others. He cut Féolan off before he could start, his voice bleak.

"We have to leave. I know."

It had been a long time since Derkh had had to call on the harsh self-discipline instilled in him since childhood. He called on it now, every ounce and drop of it, to turn his back on the woman he loved. They had come to save the children. He would not be the one to endanger them.

Just let her be safe, he prayed. I won't ask more.

CHAPTER TWENTY-SIX

Y OLENKA'S GOLDEN EYES WERE PITILESS as she stared down at the man dying on the floor. He thrashed and retched. A thin greenish foam collected in the corners of his mouth.

She was already too late to join the group, she knew. It was the price. She was sorry about Derkh—but she had waited long, long years to watch this man's death, and she would not cut it short by one breath.

More than ten years, it was, since her little sister had been taken by Turga's men. Aliri was not fiery and strong like her big sister, but a delicate and gentle soul. Yolenka still remembered her mother's sobbing broken voice as she told how she had screamed and fought to get to her daughter, how Aliri had wailed in terror as she was carried off. The man who had pulled the little girl onto his horse struck her so violently to silence her that her head snapped nearly off its stalk; the blood had trickled from her mouth and she had slumped limp across the saddle. That was the sight that tortured her mother's memory ever after.

It should have been me, Yolenka had thought to herself. If I had not gone off to train with Riko, they would have taken me. Or if they took us both, I could have looked after her. For years she carried this guilty misery in her soul. And then, overnight it seemed, the guilt was transformed into hate.

She had purchased the poison in secret years ago and carried it with her for so long she was afraid it had lost its potency. Apparently not. Turga was taking some time to die, but there seemed little doubt that he would. Cautious though he was, Turga was like most men: a few kisses, a little wine, and he lost his sense of danger. It had been easy to take a turn pouring the drinks, to flick open the tiny chamber in her ring and add the murky liquid hidden within. Yolenka would have shared the drink with him to assuage his fears if it had come to that, but it had not. He had reached for the wine greedily, and now he lay before her, racked with convulsions and growing steadily more feeble.

Yolenka bent close to his ear. "Do you hear me, Turga? Do your ears work still?" His eyes rolled at her, but he made no reply. He had all he could do just to draw breath.

She spat, square in his face. "This is for my sister. And this"— she straightened and kicked him, hard, putting all her dancer's muscle behind it—"is for all the other children you have robbed of their lives."

She waited until he was dead and then dragged him under the puffy splendor of his silk covers, on his side, face to the wall. With a pillow tucked tenderly under his head, he looked comfortable enough. If she was lucky, his death might not be discovered until late morning.

She muttered a brief prayer to the Great Mother of All. Muki had her Vengeful Guise, like all mothers. If the Mother's blessing stayed with her, Yolenka thought she had a good chance of being well away by dawn

"Where's this lot going, so late at night?"

The head guard, Rayf, called his mates away from their *reneñas* to the gatehouse window overlooking the courtyard.

"My turn, mind," muttered Cavran, reluctant to leave the game. They all three watched the peddlers' mule, heavy caravan in tow, plod across the yard toward the gate. There was nothing for it but to go out and meet them.

Two men sat up front with the reins. A third paced beside the wagon. Where was the dancing girl, wondered Cavran? As far as he'd heard, the rest were foreigners, with hardly a word of Tarzine between them. He considered offering to translate, as he had on ship with those kids—and held off. Let them sweat a bit first, he thought, trying to talk their way out of here. Might be worth a laugh.

The tall one answered the challenge and spoke the words clearly enough.

"The Gray Veil," he said. "Did die. Turga say leave."

The three guards eyed each other, caught between alarm and confusion. Was one of the peddlers dead of the Veil, wondered Cavran. Maybe the dancer?

"I heard that remedy woman was treating Turga's slave girl," Rayf muttered. He raised his voice again to the peddlers' spokesman.

"Who's dead? Explain."

"Small mans…I don't know words," the tall one—he was the musician, Cavran remembered now—said. "You look?" And he climbed down from the wooden bench and opened the back of the caravan.

Cavran and his mate edged backward. Rayf had started this—let him finish it.

"Damn rabbit hearts." Give him full credit, as head guard, Rayf did his job. He stalked over to the caravan. Cavran was unperturbed by the senior man's disgust. If the travelers were infected, there was no point in all three exposing themselves.

"Ah, great Kiar's axe." Rayf's retreat from the wagon was a little too hasty to be dignified.

"That remedy woman's in there with two bodies!" Rayf rubbed a hand along his night-stubbled jawline as though to erase the sight. "Little bodies, by the looks of them. Gotta be those two kids. Wielder's wood, I wondered why they had the whole damn hallway blocked off."

He looked up at the musician, still standing patiently by the caravan.

"Get them out of here!" he said. "The lot of you, clear out!"

The tall musician nodded gravely, climbed back into the seat and coaxed the mule back into motion while Cavran unbarred and swung open the gate.

Cavran had to fight the urge to hold his breath as the doomed wagon rumbled past. Stupid, that was. If the bloody Veil was loose in the stronghold, not breathing now was hardly going to save him. Every man's health was in the hands of his Maker now.

The peddlers, though—they had cause to be worried, poor buggers. No wonder they looked strained. What would they do with the load of death they carried, and with the woman who might well carry the seeds of sickness even now? Cavran watched the two men's faces as they passed and was surprised to see relief brighten the expression of the shorter sunburned one.

"I wasn't sure they would buy it," he said to the musician—at least that's what it sounded like. Hard to tell in a foreign language, and with the noise of the wheels. Something about buying, anyway, which made sense for traders he supposed. And then he was looking at the back end of the wagon, the end that opened onto two corpses that could mean trouble for Turga's whole settlement. Turga was right to get them out fast, thought Cavran. Maybe that would be the end of it. He swung shut the heavy gate and fitted the square-cut bars into place.

The *reneñas* game was waiting. But something nagged at him.

Do even traders talk about their profits at a time like this, with plague a dark presence in their midst? What was sold, exactly, and who was *they*? And why that relieved face?

The whole business smelled queer, now that he thought about it. He took the steps into the gatehouse slowly, trying to weigh the cost of speaking up or keeping mum.

"C'mon man, it's your turn."

Cavran entered the gatehouse and shook his head at his *reneñas* partner. "They said Turga ordered them to leave, right? I think we should check it out with him."

MATTHIEU HAD KEPT still as a log when the guard looked inside. He breathed the way Gabrielle had taught him, lightly into his belly where the blanket was bunched and fastened so no tell-tale chest movement would give them away. He had given no thought to his discomfort then, his mind taken up with the danger of the moment and the fear that Madeleine would stir or cry out in her fever. Gabrielle must have done something, though, for Madeleine lay quiet, and the man believed.

But now—now that Gabrielle's whispers had told him they

were safely through the gates and on the road—the scratchy hot shroud had become a quiet torture. Sweat trickled from Matthieu's hairline and armpits and pooled under his head and shoulders. The air under the blanket was thick and sluggish in his lungs.

He was determined not to complain. Gabrielle would let him out when she thought it was safe—and soon enough, she did. The inside of the wagon was dark and smoky, lit only by a tiny lamp fastened to a wall bracket. Gabrielle had unwrapped Madeleine first, he saw, and although she smiled and told him he'd done well, he could see her thoughts were with his sister. He asked if he could go to his dad.

"I think he's riding on the footboard at the back," she said. "Poke your head out, and you can ask him."

Matthieu was about to push back the drape that kept the wind and dust out of the caravan when a terrible thought struck him.

"Gabrielle," he asked.

Her eyes stayed on Madeleine. "Mmm?"

"Could I have it too, what Maddy has? Could I give it to everyone else?"

This time her eyes rested on him, fully present.

"Have you felt sick at all, Matthieu? Even just like you're getting a cold?"

He shook his head. "I got hot and kind of headachy in the blanket, but, no, I've been fine."

"Good. But you know what? C'mon back here, and let me check you out anyway."

Gabrielle's cool fingers cradled each side of his jawline. His neck grew warm and a little tingly under her hands. When he and Madeleine were smaller and both sick with the flu, they had tried to describe the feeling when their aunt "worked" on them. "Like sunshine inside you," his sister had tried. "A cat purring over your sore places" had been Matthieu's attempt, but Madeleine had thought that silly. Matthieu stood by his younger words, though—the sensation still reminded him of the happy soothing feeling of a cat purring in his lap.

Gabrielle opened her eyes, and her smile told him she had found nothing. "I'd bet all Derkh's silver that you're fine," she said, and Matthieu didn't waste time asking her what silver she was talking about.

DOMINIC AND MATTHIEU trudged along the road beside the mule, hand in hand. The moon rode high overhead, spilling a wash of light before their feet. To each side of them, the land was black and still. At home, Matthieu had pronounced holding hands "babyish" and refused to do it with anyone but his little brother. Today they both held tight. If they could have kept up with the cart while walking wrapped in each other's arms, they would have.

Dominic would have liked nothing better than to give his whole heart and mind over to his son—but they were not safe yet. Sooner or later Turga would discover what they had done and send horsemen after them.

"Papa?"

Dominic looked down to see worried brown eyes trained on his face. He reached out a hand to tousle curls that were no longer there and smoothed it along the top of his son's head instead. "What is it, Matthieu?"

"Is this all we have to escape? The mule? Don't we need something faster?"

Dominic nodded. "If they come after us, we'll have to fight them and take their horses. That's why Féolan just ran ahead, to look for a likely place. Did you meet Turga at all, Matthieu? Do you think he'll come after us?"

Matthieu shrugged. "I didn't really see him, but—yeah. He thought he was going to get lots of money for..." The boy's voice faltered.

Gods curse the man, Dominic thought, feeling the rush of anger to his head. He shook it off. He needed clarity now, not drama.

"Madeleine's sickness, he seemed pretty scared of it," he suggested. "He might not be anxious to expose more of his men to it."

He had meant it to be reassuring. But Matthieu, he saw, had been worrying over this as well.

"What's wrong with Maddy, Papa? It seemed like she just had a cold, but now she's so sick."

"They call it the Gray Veil. It's a bad sickness, Matthieu, and that's why people here are afraid of it. But they don't have Gabrielle to heal them, and Maddy does."

They were interrupted by Féolan's return.

"There's a perfect spot to set up not far from here," he said, "lots of cover and a sudden approach."

"Time to make our bets, then," said Dominic. "Are we pursued, or are we not?" The decision was his to make, but if there was one thing he had learned in his years of governing it was how to take counsel.

"Derkh? What do you think?"

Derkh, guiding the mule, kept his eyes on the road. "I don't know about Turga. But Yolenka is Tarzine, and she'd go after anybody who took something she thought was hers." Though his voice was firm and neutral, the tension in his posture was telling. He's got it bad for that girl, Dominic thought, realizing for the first time just how hard it must have been for Derkh to leave without her.

"Féolan?"

"I agree. He's leery of the Gray Veil, that's certain, but he's a warlord. He holds power by being bold and predatory. He won't allow foreign riffraff to amble off with his plunder."

Dominic nodded. His own assessment followed the same lines. It might be wise, given Madeleine's condition, for Turga to let them go and save his stronghold from further exposure. But it would look like weakness, and men who rule through fear cannot afford weakness.

"Then let's get to work."

CHAPTER TWENTY-SEVEN

S O HE HAD BEEN RIGHT to be suspicious. But by the Hewer's blood, Cavran had never dreamed of murder, not by that ragtag little group! He had been braced, rather, for Turga's wrath at being awakened, had almost turned back when Turga's guard told him the boss was asleep after a night of drinking. But he had persevered, and when he explained his suspicions—suspicions that had sounded so flimsy at the guardhouse that he had tried to follow Rayf's advice and bury them in a few rounds of betting tiles—he had gained an unexpected ally.

Turga's night guard had frowned. "That don't sound right," he said. "I don't see how he could have even got news of those slaves—he was shut up with that dancing woman all night. She only left a short while ago."

And so they had knocked and shouted and then entered Turga's private chambers, and found him not deaf from drink, as they expected, but dead.

Now, while Turga's guard went to rouse Zhirak, Turga's second man and likely successor, Cavran's mind raced into the future. The death of a warlord brought danger—and sometimes opportunity—to his men. Zhirak would not assume Turga's power unchallenged. And as soon as word got out, neighboring warlords would attack, sensing weakness in the leadership like a shark senses blood.

Where would Cavran be when the blood stopped flowing?

He pondered this as he made his way back to the gatehouse. He had some faith in Zhirak—the man didn't have Turga's style, but he was smart and courageous, not to mention a one-man powerhouse in a fight. As a betting man, he put his coin with Zhirak. And that meant he wanted to be right at his side, under his protection, as soon as possible.

Cavran was a recent recruit of Turga's, a former merchant sailor hired for his knowledge of the Krylian language and coastline. He was still low in the ranks, but if he were to prove his worth now he could rise, and fast. How better than to bring back Turga's assassins, along with his slaves (alive and kicking, Cavran would bet on that too) and their gold? He would need men…horses. And weapons. He was not authorized to order up a posse, but if there was ever a time to bend the rules, this was it.

A sudden doubt stopped his steps. What about the girl? She was not long gone from Turga's chamber, surely still within the walls. Should he not go after her? His lip turned in scorn—all those men, and they sent the Tarzine woman to do the dirty job.

No, he would let Zhirak deal with her. Cavran's business was with the foreign thieves, the ones *he* had suspected when the others were gulled.

He was trotting now, his purpose clear. Men. Horses. Weapons. They would sweep down on those ill-begotten vagabonds and teach them the folly of cheating a pirate warlord.

MATTHIEU BRUSHED AT THE mosquito feasting on his neck, not allowing himself to slap, and shifted his weight to one side, trying to ease away from the stone poking up against his hip. He'd been lying there a long time, long enough for every rock, stick and root to make itself felt. Long enough for the air to lose its dense blackness and soften to gray. He had even heard a few sleepy tentative birdcalls, but the road was still quiet. Maybe they weren't even coming. Maybe they'd guessed wrong, busted the wheel for nothing and now they'd be stranded.

It hadn't been that easy to find a place to hide, especially in the dark. The torches from the caravan made only small puddles of light. This low pocket of land had a lot more trees than the rest of the countryside, but most were thin and scrubby. The one Matthieu peered through, however, had been ripped from the ground in some former storm, and its once buried roots now thrust their snaky fingers into the air. The solid center was broad and high enough to shield him even if he sat up, while the gaps in the twined wood made perfect peepholes.

The short sword his father had given him lay snug along his side. He eased his hand down to curl around the hilt. "Just for your own protection," Papa had stressed, and given firm orders to stay out of sight. Still, he hadn't made him go off into the woods with Gabrielle and Madeleine, had allowed him to stay within view of the road. If anything did happen, Matthieu would see it.

FÉOLAN, STATIONED BEFORE the bend in the road, heard the hoofbeats long before there was anything to be seen. As he loped back to the others, he took a last look at their handiwork: The approaching horsemen would come down a slope to a hairpin turn, then to the cart canted off at the roadside with a broken wheel. He nodded, satisfied: It was a believable scene. And there wouldn't be time for them to think twice. He raised his arm to signal their pursuers' approach.

YOLENKA'S KNOCK ON the barracks door was soft but persistent. The last thing she wanted was to wake the whole lot of them.

Finally, she heard a mumbled curse and footfalls. The door opened.

"What?" The man's sleep-rumpled face went slack with surprise when he saw her; then it rearranged itself into a bleary grin. "Helloo-oo. Looking for me?"

Yolenka smiled apologetically. "Sadly, no. I'm sorry to disturb. I need to speak to Gurtemin. Is he there?"

"Course he's here, he's sleepin' like the rest of us." Surly again. "'Cepting me, that is."

Yolenka laid a placating hand on his arm. "I'm sorry. I think he will not mind waking up for me. And"—with a little caress, she laid a gold coin into his hand—"of course I will make it worth your while as well."

"Mmm." Cheerier now. "Hang on, then."

Gurtemin, one of the gatehouse guards Yolenka had made it her business to meet, was more alert than his predecessor when he came to the door. He tugged his fingers through bed-tousled hair and leaned against the doorframe in a pose he no doubt imagined as rakish.

"Yolenka. Couldn't keep away from me, is it?"

It was easy to get him outside into the privacy of the compound.

"Gurtemin, I need your help. My partners"—she spat angrily—"my so-called partners, have left. They took our profits and lit out. And they've lifted some of Turga's possessions and left me to shovel their dung."

Gurtemin's bony hands lifted in the gesture of warding.

"You got me up for this? It's not my problem." Mouth drawn down in displeasure, he made to turn away.

"Gurtemin, wait! You haven't heard all."

A pause. A sigh. And he faced her once more.

"Tell, then. But make it fast. You're a woman to dream on, but you got no claim on me."

"Yet I think you will be interested in my offer." Yolenka smiled lazily and drew close to him, speaking low so he would have to bend toward her to hear, as she laid out her plan.

CHAPTER TWENTY-EIGHT

HOW MANY WERE THERE? Hopefully not as many as the horses Dominic had seen in the stable. They would have little chance of success if they were wildly outnumbered.

It all hinged on Turga's beliefs about them, Dominic decided. He didn't think, even yet, that anyone had suspected their true identity. As long as Turga still believed he was after tradesmen—bold dishonest tradesmen to be sure, but not trained warriors—he was unlikely to bother mustering a large force. The speed with which they had been pursued argued that a quick response, rather than strength, had been uppermost in Turga's mind.

Worry for his children—Mother of all, Madeleine looked so ill!—washed through Dominic like a sudden chill. He should have made Matthieu go with Gabrielle, someplace where there was no chance the boy would try to join in the fight.

Dominic clamped down on his mind before the image of Matthieu sprouting a sword through his side could become fully formed. He could hear the hoofbeats himself now, coming fast. There was no room in battle for any other thoughts. How strange, he thought, that to protect his children he must forget about them now.

He checked his bow one last time. He and Féolan were crouched across the road from the caravan. They had one shot only, with any luck disabling two men, before they must leap out and grapple directly with the remaining horsemen. The Tarzines must not be allowed time to retreat back down the road or to take cover. Derkh, untrained in archery, would attack with his sword from the other side, closing in behind the Tarzines as soon as the arrows had been loosed. If the two bowmen did not join him in an instant, he would not last long against mounted opponents.

And then they were upon them. The pounding hoofbeats slowed for the sharp turn, and he could see their dark shapes: three, four, six men. More than he would like, but not impossible odds. Their horses danced in place while the men pulled up to take in the scene. In the dawn half-light Dominic could just make out the flash of teeth as they exchanged cocky smirks. Good, he thought. That's just how I want you to feel. Imagine how you will thunder upon us as we limp helpless down the road just ahead.

As the men kicked their horses forward and drew even with the caravan, Dominic eased up from behind the boulder that hid him and trained his sights on the broad back of the nearest horseman, obligingly turned his way as the man studied the broken wagon wheel. He couldn't ask for a better target.

HIS PAPA SHOT first and hit his mark square. Matthieu had to bite his lips to hold back a yell of triumph. But his excitement was short-lived, drowned by the cry of the shot man. This was not like the confused battle Matthieu had seen before, the air full of shouts and battle screams and vague dark figures. This scream pierced the silence, filling his ears, and he saw the grimacing face as it fell, lips drawn back like a dog's.

A heartbeat later, Féolan's bow sang out. His shot was not so clear, and his target's horse, rearing in alarm at just that moment, saved its rider from a lethal hit. The arrow sank into his thigh, painful but not disabling.

The bowstring twanged again. His father? No, Dominic was already running in with his sword drawn. Féolan then, impossibly fast. But his opponent was fast too and quick-witted despite his wound. Anticipating the second shot, perhaps, or reacting with cat-like speed to the sound, he threw himself down and sideways in the saddle. The arrow meant for his heart drove into his shoulder.

It was enough. Féolan darted in, pulled the wounded man to the ground and vaulted into the saddle.

Where was Derkh? And his father? Matthieu's eyes scanned frantically—and his legs went weak with alarm.

They were in trouble. Derkh had rushed forward as planned, only to find himself facing not swords but spears, a seeming thicket of them. Dominic was at his side, having somehow made his way across the road. With the height of the mounted Tarzines and the long reach of their weapons, there was no effective way to attack. Instead, Derkh and Dominic were pinned behind the cover of the caravan, unable to break free without being skewered by a spear hurled at close range.

Féolan yanked the lance free from its clip on the saddle. Three men hedging in Derkh and Dominic and only one left against him—but that one had already kicked his horse to a canter with his arm cocked back for the throw. Féolan dropped the reins, drew his sword left-handed. It seemed to Matthieu he became a statue, frozen in all that turbulent clamor. His opponent grinned, avid, sure of his prey. But just as he loosed the spear, Féolan's horse side-stepped left and his sword swung in an arc, deflecting the spearhead past his right shoulder. The Tarzine came on, caught in his own momentum, and Féolan's spear flashed. A final brutal sword stroke and it was done.

It was three on three now. The Tarzines, Matthieu saw, were no longer grinning. He guessed they hadn't expected any real danger, only a bunch of scared runaways. But they still had the advantage in horses and weapons.

If Féolan had his bow...But it was on the other side of the road from Matthieu—no way to get to it unnoticed. Was there nothing he could do but watch helplessly?

In a chiggers game, this is where you would need your hidden token, he thought. Too bad we don't have one. But the idea stayed with him. In a way, this *was* like a chiggers game, wasn't it? Looking at it that way helped to quiet the scared feelings that scrabbled around in his mind, making it so hard to think.

Matthieu's eyes narrowed. He looked again at the scene below him. It was a chiggers board...a very large, very unusual chiggers board.

THREE MEN DOWN! Cavran's hope of reward for his daring action had fallen into the shit pit. Even assuming the boy was still healthy, he would hardly compensate for their losses. He would do better to snatch the boy and take off, sell him and keep the profit for himself. Of course his colleagues might have something to say to that.

First they had to finish off this lot. They had them now, he was sure, but he had underestimated them badly before and was not about to make the same mistake twice. The two trapped behind the wagon were hardly cowering in fear. And the other, the skinny musician—he was fast as a snake and just as deadly.

Cavran edged his horse toward the back end of the caravan and motioned to his fellow to go around the front. They would squeeze the two on foot between them, finish them off first while the musician was kept at bay.

A sudden noise in the wooded hill above them caught his attention.

"It's the boy!" shouted his mate. "Will I go for him?"

"Hold your ground," Cavran roared. "He's got nowhere to run to—we'll pick him up after this work is done." Sure, run off with the prize and leave me outnumbered, he thought. Not likely.

"DOMINIC, THEY'RE COMING around to make their move." Derkh shifted position, keeping his face square to the horseman, but he didn't harbor much hope of dodging the spear when it finally flew. The Tarzines would have to ride into the brush at the side of the road and search around a bit for a clear flight path, but it wouldn't take them long. "I don't relish a headlong flight into the bush with horses on my tail."

"Got your knife, Derkh?" Dominic had already switched his sword to his left hand and eased the Elvish blade, now at his waist, from its sheath. It might be his last hope now.

"Yeah, right here. I guess it's the only thing left to do, but, dark gods, it's a bugger of a throw." To hit a man at such a height, while trying to avoid a flying spear? Even when he was in peak training form that would have been beyond Derkh's skill.

"I was thinking the horses," Dominic muttered. "I know we need them, but we can lose a couple."

Derkh nodded agreement. Of course. Horses made an easier target, and if they could manage to make the horses stumble or rear that might just gain them an opening.

CHAPTER TWENTY-NINE

MATTHIEU SCRAMBLED THROUGH the scrubby brush. He ran at an angle, away from the road and back toward Turga's. There it was—the big outcropping of rock.

"Gabrielle!" She was sitting with Madeleine's head in her lap, but thank the gods not in her spooky trance.

"Matthieu, what on—"

"I need the mule. There's no time to explain. They're in trouble down there, and I have an idea. Gabrielle, just trust me—it's not that dangerous, and it might help. But it has to be now."

Uncertain green eyes rested on him while Matthieu squirmed with impatience. Then they cleared, and Gabrielle nodded.

"Go then. But for pity's sake, Matthieu, be careful."

He untied the mule and began urging her through the woods. She was happy to follow—she didn't like this rough country and sensed the road ahead. Matthieu aimed to reach it just ahead of the hairpin turn. He should be able to walk right onto it and still be out of sight.

He gave a quick glance up and down as they reached the roadside, but there was no time for real caution. If there were more men in wait there, they were scuppered anyway. He led the mule into the road, faced her toward the caravan and skirted around to her back end.

"Sorry, girl," he murmured. And quickly, before he could get cold feet, he drew his sword and stabbed her in the flank.

Searing pain branded his thigh. He sprawled in the dust, clutching his leg to his chest, while behind his eyes the great black shape of a hoofprint flared and throbbed.

"Serves me right," he croaked.

But his plan, such as it was, had worked. The mule had bolted down the road in a lather. Maybe she would actually crash into them. Matthieu hoped so. He hoped it wasn't too late to matter.

He hoped his leg still worked.

DOMINIC KEPT HIS EYES trained on the approaching horseman while he hefted the weight of the knife in his hand. It was years since he had practiced knife-throwing and never with a blade like this. It was slim, beautifully balanced, but longer than he was used to. That would mean slower rotations—so he would need a little more distance to get a stick. And he needed to get his throw in ahead of the spear cast. His fingers closed down into the hammer grip that General Fortin had taught him. He would aim at the broadest part of the horse's neck. Harder to miss.

The Tarzine coming at him hefted the spear back in preparation for his throw. Dominic's arm swung up. A screaming bray shattered the air, a large brown shape shot clattering and skidding around the bend, and the Tarzine's taut features dissolved into slack-mouthed surprise. A mule—*their* mule—streaming blood and already out of control from the sharp turn, screamed again in panic as it saw the obstacles before it, tried to swerve, slewed its back end into the Tarzine's horse and lashed out with a frightened kick. The Tarzine yelled in pain and clutched at his calf—and Dominic had his chance.

He eyeballed the distance, took two quick steps back and snapped his arm in a smooth arc. The knife sailed away, made two lazy turns and sank into the horse's broad neck.

The horse collapsed at the knee and pitched forward. Dominic's sword was at the Tarzine's throat before the poor beast came to rest. He hauled the man off the saddle and shoved him up against the wagon with the long blade pressed across his neck.

Over his own heavy breathing, he heard the scuffle and grunt of fighting. Derkh and Féolan had followed his lead, but they had not had so good an opening as he.

This time there was no avoiding it; he would have to kill the man in cold blood. He couldn't stand here waiting while his friends were hard pressed.

Gritting his teeth, he took a firm, two-handed grip on his sword.

"Wait! I call them off."

Dominic stared, his brain not quite believing his ears.

"You speak Krylaise?"

The man gave a tiny careful nod around the sword. "I stop them."

Easing back just slightly on the pressure, Dominic said, "Do it."

A BRIGHT BLAZING sun popped over the eastern tree line and washed the world in lavish pink as Dominic hoisted Matthieu onto Gabrielle's horse and settled him in front of his aunt. There were enough horses that the boy could have ridden alone, but the swollen livid lump on his thigh argued against it. Dominic wanted badly to have Matthieu on his own horse, but Derkh had pointed out that would leave only one trained fighter unencumbered. Madeleine rode with Féolan though Gabrielle was loath to give her up. The girl was not much smaller than her aunt, too heavy for Gabrielle to support securely at a gallop.

Dominic sent the Tarzines down the road on foot, their wounded man slung over the mule.

The only debate was about what to do with the extra horse. Dom was not anxious to bring it along—a tether would be nothing but a hindrance in case of attack—nor did he want to provide the Tarzines with swift transportation back to Turga. It would certainly overtake them if he set it free.

In the end, they waited until the Tarzines were well away, hobbled the horse and left it to make its slow way home.

PUSHING THE HORSES, but not exhausting them, they were able to make the journey from Rath Turga to Niz Hana in one long hard day. It was not fast enough for Gabrielle's liking; she could feel Madeleine weakening with each slow mile and fretted against the lazy dogleg road that looped inland before angling back to the coast. Once, at a nameless crossroads settlement, Dominic called a halt to buy bread and ale at the tiny market. Gabrielle spent every minute of their brief stop sitting with Madeleine, struggling to check the advances the disease had made through the morning. Féolan's efforts to lend Madeleine strength were helping, but they were no substitute for Gabrielle's powers.

She had no appetite for the rough round of bread Féolan pressed on her, but she chewed it dutifully as they traveled. "Stoke your fire," she remembered her father urging. "No heat without fuel."

They all quickened with hope as their road branched left, back toward the coast. Surely if they had not been overtaken by now, they would reach Niz Hana safely. The road sloped downhill, gradually taking them out of the dry uplands and into the green low pocket of lusher country that surrounded the harbor town.

Matthieu whooped in triumph as they passed through the town gates, the sound so infectious that everyone but Derkh had to laugh. Derkh was somber, his dark brows creased. Gabrielle caught a trace, like a scent carried on the wind, of the stew of feelings behind his frown: fear, loss, anger, determination. Love. He was deeply, irrevocably in love with Yolenka, she realized, and she felt her own gust of anger against the Tarzine woman. What was she playing at? If she wanted to stay in her own homeland there was no blame to it, but to disappear without a word of explanation...

They were at the harbor now, and there was the ship at the end of the pier, waiting as promised. Had anything ever looked so lovely as that ship? She would settle Madeleine into the captain's room and get to work undisturbed and heal her niece, and the ship would carry them home.

CHAPTER THIRTY

THE CAPTAIN PLANTED HIMSELF in front of them, barring the way, and folded his arms across his chest. "I will not have the Veil on my ship."

Féolan tried to gather his thoughts and words. He was tired from the long ride, distracted by Gabrielle's worry. He would normally enjoy the challenge of a new language, but not when lives hung on his eloquence. Not with this dull fog in his head.

"Dominic, would you take Madeleine?" He passed the sick girl carefully to her father. It put him at another disadvantage with the captain, trying to argue with his arms full.

Dominic and Gabrielle stood behind him, alarmed and frustrated. Not Derkh. Derkh had left them shipside. "You're safe now," he had said. "I'm staying. Yolenka might make it here after all. If need be, I'll go back for her." Féolan didn't know how Derkh would fare, returning to Turga's stronghold with hardly a word of Tarzine—or how Yolenka would respond if he arrived there. But he missed Derkh's steady quiet presence.

Féolan turned back to the captain. "You agreed to sail us," he insisted. "We paid. You know we came for the children."

"I didn't agree to carry the damn plague!" The man's eyebrows drew down in a glowering line. "I won't put my men at risk."

"Féolan." It was Gabrielle. "Tell him I will stay with Madeleine in the cabin and not come out. We will stay away from his men."

Féolan stumbled through the proposal. The captain seemed, for a moment, to soften. Then the eyebrows jutted down again, and he widened his stance.

"What about Turga? Did you kill the pirate?"

"No." Féolan didn't hide his surprise. "That was not our...not why we came here."

"Bleeding eyes of mighty Milor." The captain hawked onto his own deck in disgust. "What you bring me here is trouble. Disease on my ship. Turga alive and on your tail. When I return here, what do you think will be waiting for me? He won't rest until he puts me out of business or under the waves!"

"He will rest." The voice was commanding as a clarion. "He will rest until the end of days."

Féolan turned to see Yolenka, her gauzy costume sweat-stained and dusty, hair a windblown fury, stalk past him and stop just short of the captain's face. She jabbed a finger into his chest, and he took an alarmed half-step backward before catching himself. Féolan found himself feeling a little sorry for the man.

"Turga is dead." Yolenka bowed and swept her hands open in an ironic exaggerated gesture of bounty. "A gift for you." She straightened and her voice grew hard. "We have paid you gold to grow fat on and swept the seas clean of your worst predator. Now it is for you to hold up your end and carry these children home."

She swept her eyes over him with frank scorn. "I did not think to see such cowardice in a Tarzine captain."

All eyes, crew and passenger, were on the captain. He blustered and bridled, stung by the insult, groping after a reply that would salvage his pride and his men's respect.

Yolenka let him stew in his own anger. Then her features softened, became almost pleading, and she touched his arm hesitantly.

"Your pardon," she said. "I spoke wrongly. There is no cowardice in protecting your crew."

The captain, on the verge of smacking her arm away, stopped in confusion. The poor lout, thought Féolan. She's playing him like a bag of *reneñas*. Yolenka continued, all humble supplication.

"They are children. They have suffered great evil, and it is due to them that Turga is killed. Now their fate rests in your hands. Will you not save them?"

Agonizing moments ticked by. The captain shifted his weight, scratched at the stubble under his chin. Met Yolenka's liquid golden gaze. Straightened briskly.

"I'll clean out my things," he announced. "But…" He pointed a finger and swept it stiffly across the little group. "You lot will eat and sleep on deck. And any one of you has the least complaint, even a bloody hangnail, you're confined to the cabin."

YOLENKA PERCHED ON a coil of rope, her ruined finery tucked around her legs, and systematically worked a comb through her tangles. Derkh sat beside her, feeling the movement of the ship underneath him—a familiar motion this time, cheering even. The seas were calm as sunset approached, the breeze billowing the sails playfully. They had just lost sight of land. Derkh watched Yolenka's fingers move briskly through the strands of hair, let his eyes travel over her golden features. What if she had not returned? He still felt weak from the fear of it, and from the relief that had washed through him when he first caught sight of her galloping breakneck down the narrow street on a lathered horse, people scattering in her wake. His lips curled into a private grin at the memory.

"What? You are smiling because dinner arrives, I hope." Yolenka scowled. "Will this captain never feed us? I am near to falling down starved."

"When did you eat last?" Derkh was hungry too—their quick midday meal had been a small chink in a yawning gap.

"Not anytime this day."

"Yolenka..." Where to start? Maybe not the beginning—he wasn't sure he was ready for the story of Turga's death. "How did you get out of there?"

Yolenka glinted up at him. "There is guard I know. I make a deal."

Eternal night. Did she have to joke about it like that? Heat rose in his face, and Derkh was glad for the sunburn that hid his angry flush. I'm too jealous, he thought bleakly. I will never survive her.

"Never mind, I don't want to—"

She laid a hand on his arm. "Stop now. Is no need for making that red face more red. I win much gold from him in *renenas*. I offer it back to him if he let me out harbor gate."

"The harbor gate?" Derkh hadn't noticed another gate.

"Yes, is gate at harbor side. Not for travelers. For ship's cargo. Is always locked except for loading times." Her look was stern now. "I have much trouble to return here. I circle around far from stronghold to escape searchers. Very rough country in darkness. I think, I never reach Niz Hana in time, you leave without me. Then when I find road again, what do I see?"

Derkh made a sudden guess, darted a look and saw in her brilliant smile that he was right.

"A broken cart, some dead men. Not you dead, is good sign. And then not much farther, I find horse, all ready for a rider."

They sat in silence for a bit, close now to the heart of what had happened between them.

"There is something else I find." Yolenka spoke so softly, her face veiled by a down-sweep of hair, that Derkh could barely make out the words. "You are not on the ship." Her voice was wondering.

He shook his head. "No," he said, "I wasn't." He waited while she hooked the sheet of hair behind her ear and raised her head to meet his eyes.

"I was ready to go back and find you," he said. "I love you. Wherever you are, that's where I want to be. I want to be your man." And then, because it was Yolenka and because of what he had endured in the past week, he thought he had better be perfectly clear. "Your only man."

"You *are* my only man," she said, and for once there was no hint of teasing in her tone, but a low fierce passion. And she twined her arms around his neck, and right there on the busy deck he kissed her, and he didn't let her loose until the whistle finally called them to eat.

The black water closed over her head and poured cold and oily into her mouth. It cut off all air, all light, and pushed her deep below the surface. She sank into utter blackness, drowned. At the bottom, Luc waited for her, his white throat gaping and closing in the current like gills.

With a harsh rasp Madeleine sucked at the air, pulling it
through the painful swollen flap of her throat and sobbing it out
again. She was weeping, and the more she gasped and cried the
more her throat clenched shut. It was her dream all over again,
only without any water.

"Maddy, easy now."

Aunt Gabrielle. Madeleine felt the woman's arms about her,
felt her warm calm presence enter her.

"I can't breathe!" She heaved, heard the breath rattle grudgingly into her lungs. "I can't—"

"Nice and slow, love. Try like this." Gabrielle adjusted
Madeleine's position, tipped her head back just a little in the
crook of her arm. Something seemed to relax in her throat. "Little
soft breaths."

She needed more than little breaths, needed great rushes of
air to chase away the dream, but Gabrielle breathed with her
and as she grew calmer the air flowed back. Panic softened to
confused sorrow.

"I'm dying," she murmured. "Like Luc. His throat opened
up, and he died. Because of me. My throat is closed up, and I'll
die too. Like Luc…"

"No, Madeleine." Gabrielle's voice was firm, like her mother's
almost. "You are not going to die. We are going to keep your
throat open, and you will live."

Madeleine didn't know if that was true. She knew she had
never been so sick, that "sore throat" didn't remotely capture what
was wrong with her. She thought if she drifted back to the dark,
not-quite-sleep that filled her mind with bizarre dreams and bright
wheeling colors, she might not awaken. She tried to hang onto

her aunt's voice, but she was so tired. And her throat—she could not endure the sensation, not just the pain but the horror of it, her own tender tissue become monstrous.

Gabrielle's voice faded away, but Madeleine felt the warm bright light flooding into her and knew her aunt was with her. Here was a better place to go than the dark dreams of her illness. She hung on until she felt cradled in Gabrielle's warm presence, and then she gave herself up to sleep.

CHAPTER THIRTY-ONE

YOLENKA TAPPED ON THE CABIN door and pushed it open. "Gabrielle?"

It was dark in the little room, just one wall lamp casting a small pool of light. Yolenka could make out Gabrielle's form sitting close by the girl's bed. She was hunched over her patient, head drooping.

Fallen asleep, thought Yolenka. Like Féolan. Not used to staying up all night.

She laid down her tray and lit another lamp. Then she crossed the floor and laid a hand on Gabrielle's shoulder, shook it gently.

"Gabrielle, wake up! I bring dinner."

She felt the other woman start under her hand. Gabrielle straightened. She looked bleary.

"Sorry to wake you. Féolan asked me to make sure you ate." Yolenka smiled. "Is good. Captain get fresh stores at Niz Hana market."

"Well…" Gabrielle seemed reluctant, her gaze turning back to Madeleine. "Yes, I guess I had better, at that. Thanks."

She ate, as they all had, with the steady indiscriminate efficiency of the very hungry. Neither of them spoke while Gabrielle loaded in the first restorative mouthfuls.

"Where's Féolan?" Gabrielle asked.

"He say he is very tired and is going early to his bed," answered Yolenka.

Gabrielle's spoon paused on its way to her mouth and her brows creased, but she said nothing. Yolenka shrugged. "We will all join him soon. My bones are wanting death." She guessed from Gabrielle's startled glance that the expression hadn't translated very well into Krylaise. *My bones long for the grave*, meaning heavy with the need to rest. Oh well.

"How is the girl?" she asked gently. Death was, perhaps, not the best word to use in a casual expression right now.

Gabrielle shook her head. "She lost a lot of ground during that ride. The membrane on her throat is really big now. It's making it hard for her to breathe."

Yolenka nodded. "Yes, I have seen that," she said softly.

"I was thinking…" Gabrielle's features were wide awake now, her green eyes dark and intent in the lamplight. "That membrane—it could suffocate her, couldn't it?"

Yolenka gave a reluctant nod. "It happens sometimes."

"Do your healers ever remove it? If it impedes the patient's breathing, I mean? Could I not peel it away like a scab?"

Yolenka was shaking her head so hard her hair swung across her face.

"No! No, you must not!" Every child knew this. "You cannot pull aside the Veil. Beyond the Veil lies Death."

Gabrielle stared at her. "But why? What happens? Is it because of the bleeding?"

Yolenka tried to think. It was folk knowledge in her country, not something she had ever seen done. What had her mother told her? "There is bleeding, yes, but that is not the problem. Whenever it has been tried, the patient dies soon after," she said. "They say the Veil is angry and sends an evil spell on the patient, but that is just…"

Gabrielle didn't know the Tarzine word Yolenka resorted to, but she thought the phrase "country nonsense" might be close.

"But the danger is real," Yolenka insisted. "The patient loses his muscles, he shakes, his heart stops. He dies."

"His heart…" Gabrielle stared into space, her face still and closed. The remains of her dinner lay forgotten on the tiny side table. Long moments ticked by so that Yolenka wondered if her presence had become an intrusion. She had just reached across to gather up the tray, when Gabrielle spoke again.

"Yolenka, could you stay just a bit longer? I think I am close to understanding something here."

Yolenka sat down. She didn't know what Gabrielle thought she could do—children either recovered from the Veil or they didn't, and there was little the most skilled healer could do about it—but if Yolenka's sketchy knowledge could be of help, she would share it.

"You say when the Veil is removed, the patient's whole body collapses? His heart stops, his limbs…"

"Yes, is like the sickness that was in his throat goes all through him."

"Like a poison," suggested Gabrielle.

Yolenka had a vivid uncomfortable memory of Turga convulsing at her feet. What would this gentle woman think of what she had done? But her idea was right.

"Yes," she said, "I have seen poisoning. Is like that."

It was remarkable the change that had come over Gabrielle. All signs of fatigue were gone. Her face was excited, eager even.

"I need to get to work now, Yolenka," she said. "Thank you—for the food and even more for your knowledge. If my idea is right, and I pray it is, you may have just saved Madeleine."

Strange woman, thought Yolenka, as she eased the door shut. Gabrielle was slumped over the girl's bed again, to all appearances fast asleep. A ghost-chill ran up Yolenka's back. *Not asleep.* Yolenka wasn't sure what Gabrielle was doing, but it was something very different from sleep.

LIKE A POISON. Gabrielle had always felt there was some ominous power to this disease that she was not touching. What if it was a poison? What if that membrane, the Veil, was not only infecting Madeleine's throat like any other illness but making a poison that spread throughout her body? It would explain why Gabrielle made so little progress as she worked. It would explain why removing the membrane was deadly—maybe that released the poison in a great flood, and the open wound on the throat absorbed it all at once. The poison would rush through the bloodstream and enter all the vital organs...

So, she could not pull aside the Veil. But she could look behind it. She would go there and discover the secret that lay behind its protective skin.

She calmed her own urgency, let her breath come slow and steady and weightless as thistledown. She let the little room fade away, let herself float on the swell and fall of the ship. She let the healing light fill her until it seemed the glow of it could brighten the darkest deepest crevice in the ocean floor. Then she let that light pour into her niece, taking her inner vision with it.

SHE HAD IT NOW. This illness, this Gray Veil, made a double attack. Madeleine's throat infection was real and aggressive, and Gabrielle's fight to push back its spreading inflammation had not been useless. But it had not been half enough. For the hateful membrane on Madeleine's throat was also making a powerful toxin. Even knowing what to look for, it was barely discernable in the infected tissues—like looking for a glimmer of candlelight in a room full of lamps. But as the membrane grew, so did the quantity of poison that oozed from behind its leathery surface. And like a dead pigeon in a well that taints the drinking water and sickens a whole village, the poison seeped into Madeleine's blood, causing harm everywhere it traveled: heart, liver, kidneys—no wonder she had sickened so quickly!

But she was young and strong, her own body fighting hard against the invasion. There was no lasting damage yet. And Gabrielle knew what she was fighting now. For the first time in two days, she was confident that Madeleine would live.

The membrane was held at bay, and her circle of light would hold for a time. Madeleine's breath was slightly obstructed and uneasy, but not to the point of true suffocation. All of Gabrielle's power now could be trained on the evil alchemy taking place on the underside of the membrane.

The night ahead would be long—her second without rest. No sense wasting energy holding herself upright. She climbed into the narrow bed beside Madeleine, wrapped her arm around her niece's waist and sank into a deep trance.

Gabrielle looked up with a start as someone entered the room, confused by the sudden pull back to the world. Normal comings and going didn't usually disturb her, so what...?

Féolan stood in the flickering lamplight. Why does he have a scarf wrapped around his neck, she wondered vaguely, noting the bulky silhouette he made above the shoulders. It's a warm night...

"Sorry to disturb, love." Féolan's voice was a husky rasp.

"Féolan!" Gabrielle sat up in alarm, tearing free of the cobwebs that lingered from her trance. He wore no scarf, she realized. That was his neck, swollen to monstrous size right up to the ears.

"Whatever this Gray Veil is, it seems Elves are all too susceptible," said Féolan. He lay on the other bed, and Gabrielle saw how his legs buckled as they lowered to the mattress. "I woke up like this. I've come here to protect the others, but—" He held up a hand as Gabrielle scrambled to his side. "You stay with Madeleine. I felt her weaken with every mile of that journey. She needs you now." He closed his eyes and fell silent, as though that short speech had used up his strength.

CHAPTER THIRTY-TWO

PANIC WHISPERED INSIDE HER, and Gabrielle thrust it back. She could not stay the tears, though. Even by lamplight she could see that Féolan was failing before her eyes, barely hanging on to lucidity. Her eyes winced away from his swollen neck, the skin stretched and purpled, and rested on his flushed cheeks. Her hand reached out, and she felt the heat before her fingers settled on his forehead. The brilliant Elvish eyes, those eyes she loved so dearly, were dull now with pain and fever.

How could he have succumbed so quickly? In her years among the Elves, Gabrielle had seen few illnesses and rarely anything life-threatening. Most Elves had at least a touch of healing ability themselves, enough to keep at bay the coughs and fevers so common among Humans. But what if this was a completely new illness, something unlike anything they had ever been exposed to?

Gabrielle lay a hand on Féolan's chest and closed her eyes. It was hard to calm the turmoil in her mind enough to let the inner vision come to her. Precious moments ticked by as she worked on calming the ragged breath that wanted to sob rather than flow.

At last she was with him, and what she found confirmed her worst fears. The gray plaque spread deep into his throat, burrowing greedily into blood vessels and tissue. And the poison that had taken days to seep into Madeleine's system was already coursing through Féolan's body.

He was dying.

"Gabrielle." Was it his voice or his mind that called to her? He had called her once from the very brink of death, pulled her back from the last threshold beyond which there is no returning. Now it was he who wandered toward that same threshold, and still he called her.

"Gabrielle, leave me."

Never. Could I leave my own heart and soul? But even as she denied it, raged against it, she understood the choice before her. She had two patients. Neither was likely to survive without her help.

She would work on both at once. She had done it before with the twins. She would...

No. That was the healer's voice, the one that was not swayed by grief or love and thought only of the patient's chances. *The twins were alike as two peas. Healthy, except for their wounds. And even so, it was difficult. These two could not be more different.*

And had it been possible, she hadn't the strength left to do it. That was the stark brutal truth. She was exhausted.

She was weeping now, fatigue and fear and helplessness leeching the courage from her. How could this be asked of her, to leave the man she loved to die alone?

"Nay, love. No despair. It is what we all agreed."

"What do you mean?" She choked the words out between sobbing breaths. Féolan's hand stirred. He found and covered hers, the grasp weak but steady. He spoke aloud now too, though the raspy whisper must pain him.

"We came to save the children. We would all have died in a fight to rescue them. This is no different."

She felt his resolve. Even if she tried to heal him, he would use the last of his strength to shut her out. And he was right. To turn her back on Madeleine now was unthinkable.

Gabrielle laid her head on Féolan's chest and wept, her hand twined in his.

"I love you," she whispered.

"Brave Wings," he said. "Now you must fly alone. Save her, Gabrielle."

Brave Wings. The memory was a bright piercing sorrow. The words were from a wedding song Féolan had written for her, strange and beautiful and understood, as so many Elvish songs were, more in the heart than from the sense of the words:

She is brighter than the stars above,

And needs no wind to paint her brave wings.

But the memory gave her strength too, as Féolan had intended. She and Féolan had found such joy together. Maddy would have that chance too. Slowly Gabrielle sat up. She held Féolan's hand in her two. It was so hard to leave him all alone.

"I'll stay with him."

A strong blunt hand covered hers and gently freed Féolan from her grasp.

Startled, Gabrielle looked around. Derkh's face was tracked with his own tears, but his hand on her shoulder was firm.

"I won't leave him. I promise."

She had to do it now, or she never would. She gave a tiny wretched nod and turned away.

THE NIGHT CREPT ON, and Gabrielle fought for Madeleine's life. The barrier she had built around the plaque to hold back its spread along the surface of Maddy's throat did nothing to prevent the poison from penetrating through the fragile inflamed tissue behind the Veil. For that, she needed a blanket of light, a dense pool to surround the entire growth. From within this healing glow, she painstakingly sealed off the damaged flesh, pinching each tiny torn vessel closed and pushing back the dark fingers of infection. Slowly, the secret seeping pathways of the poison were blocked until Gabrielle was satisfied it was contained in a pocket behind the Veil.

That was only the first step, but she allowed herself to stop to check on Féolan. He lived still, that she knew. His life's presence was her constant companion; she would feel his death through the deepest trance. She sat on the edge of his narrow bed and tried to send him strength—*Hold on, love. Hold on till I can come to you.* But she did not dare let her mind stay with him for long. His pull was so strong; if she lingered, she might never tear herself away.

Madeleine, deep in the sleep that so often blessed Gabrielle's patients when she worked on them, drew breath in a long rattling snore. She had been gasping through that hateful growth for too long. Gabrielle smoothed Féolan's brow, kissed it, and filled his throat with light. *Just a little longer.* Two steps took her back across the tiny cabin to Madeleine. Gabrielle eased Madeleine onto her side and placed a folded towel under her cheek. She didn't want Madeleine swallowing either the plaque or its poison when the Veil came away.

Gabrielle intended to seal off the poisonous Veil and help the undamaged flesh beneath grow a protective layer of skin, just as a

wound does under its scab. Then she would simply peel the membrane away. If she did the job right, the membrane would slough
off with the seal intact, the poison contained and harmless.

Pray to all gods I'm right, she thought.

She laid her hands on either side of Madeleine's neck and
sank once more into the light.

CHAPTER THIRTY-THREE

OMINIC AWOKE IN THE FIRST CHILL half-light of dawn. Dew had settled heavily over the deck and his blanket. He was damp, stiff and cold. He eased himself up with a grimace. Matthieu lay curled in the spot beside him, burrowed under his cover. Dominic shook off his blanket and tucked it over top of his son. Not that he'd sleep much longer—once the sun rode free of the horizon and lit up the yellow sails, they would all be awake.

All didn't look to be very many, though. Only Yolenka was still on the deck. Féolan's and Derkh's rumpled blankets lay empty. Maybe they had awakened early as well. He hoped by all that was holy they had not taken ill. What if the captain had been right and the Gray Veil spread throughout the ship?

He needed to check on Madeleine. The captain frowned on anyone entering the cabin, but Dominic was her father. He would at least stick his head in the door and find out how she fared.

EVEN IN HER SLEEP Madeleine knew that the tide had turned. The trembling and twitching of her limbs first eased and then stopped altogether. The racy skip of her heart steadied. The pounding in her head, the aches that racked her body, above all the terrible weakness that made every breath an effort and sapped her will—they weren't gone, but they were fading. It was as though she had been

trapped on a sled, rushing down a long snowy slope toward a pool
so deep and icy she would sink into it like a stone and never rise
again. And then someone pulled the hand brake on the sled, and
it slowed, groaning and complaining from the strain but slowing
nonetheless, and came to rest at the edge of the pool.

And now she was making the long climb back up the hill.
With every step her body felt a little stronger and more at ease.
All except her throat. That pain was constant. For nearly two days
she had been unable to swallow, the muscles in her tongue weak
and useless. Drool had spilled down her front during that endless
pounding horse journey, and she had been too sick to care. Later
her spit had dried in her mouth and her lips had grown cracked
and parched. And none of it—not the pain, not the paralysis—was
as bad as the revulsion. She could not escape having to feel and
taste the alien thing that lay in her mouth. Her tongue knew its
leathery tough skin, the sickening press of its swelling growth.

Now, for the first time, the pain of the accidental press of
her tongue against the membrane was blunted. "Fingernails or
knives?" she and Matthieu used to ask each other, rating the
ferocity of some childish hurt. In the pain department, she was
heading back toward fingernails.

Yet the irritation of it was worse. The Veil hung in her throat,
rattling and flapping with each breath like a heavy wet curtain. It
brushed the back of her tongue, and she gagged on it, blocking
her own air. Then she couldn't stop gagging, her body trying
uselessly to eject it like a rotten chunk of meat. She struggled up
from sleep in a panic.

Patience, dear one. Soon you will be free of it. The words floated
into her mind, soothing as a mother's touch. Her throat relaxed

and opened and her breath came a little easier. Her eyelids fluttered and closed, and she slept again.

ALMOST DONE. The temptation to rush pricked at her, but Gabrielle resisted. If the seal did not hold, if the poison found some minute overlooked channel to escape through, that tiny outlet could burst open under the pressure when the Veil was removed and throw everything into jeopardy. Gabrielle's mind hovered over that word, *everything*, and she pulled it away. Don't think about what's at stake, she told herself. Think about the work.

Madeleine was restless under her hand, her sleep becoming lighter as her strength returned. The membrane was no longer embedded firmly against her throat but hung by mere threads, obstructing her airway even more than before.

Suddenly the girl choked and gagged. Gabrielle felt the fear course through her, the panic to draw air, the reflex in her throat working against her. She touched Madeleine's mind, spoke soothingly to her. Sent her light to the back of the tongue, let it fall away from the flap that brushed at it and lie flat against the jaw. Air flowed back into Madeleine's lungs, and she sighed and settled back.

"Gabrielle!"

Derkh's voice was sharp, the hand that shook her rough. "Gabrielle, wake up!"

"What is it?" Gabrielle struggled to focus her eyes, to bring her mind back to the world. Being jerked out of her healing trance was always difficult and disorienting. And tonight—this morning, rather, to judge by the thin light seeping in the cabin's tiny windows—she was slow with fatigue. It waited for her like

a silent vulture, ready to float down and take her. She shook her
head, fighting it off. There was only one reason Derkh would interrupt her.

"Féolan?"

Derkh nodded, his eyes black and staring. "He can't breathe.
Gabrielle, I think he's dying."

She flew to Féolan's bedside, not even aware of having risen.
Behind her, Madeleine coughed and gagged, choking again.
Gabrielle glanced back, agonized. Not both at once, she prayed.
I can't.

Madeleine was up on one elbow, her shoulders heaving. A
retching tearing cough shook her, and she spat a dark mass onto
the towel. A sound of pure revulsion escaped her. And then she
looked to Gabrielle, still frozen at Féolan's bedside.

"I'm okay. Look after him."

FÉOLAN FOUGHT TO draw air with everything he had. The thrashing
of his legs and hands was worse than useless, draining what stores
he had, yet he was powerless to stop it. Already his lips and fingers
tingled, starving for breath. For hours now he had survived on
small whistling passageways through the swollen mass of his throat,
using what skill he had to ease open the tissues around them and sip
miserly streams of air. Now he was in the desert, the tiniest streams
vanished in a solid wall of sand. He was dying, and he knew it.

Gabrielle's presence swept into him like the sun sailing out from
behind black clouds. She was too late, he was certain—but, oh, how
lovely to feel her near him once more. He was so sorry for the grief
she would suffer and so grateful to be with her at his life's end.

The warm light blasted into his throat, *shoving* at the swollen edges of tissue so that he could feel the sudden give, the rush of air into his grateful lungs. Then the flap closed again. *One more, Féolan.* Her voice in his head, scared but firm. Commanding him. *I'm going to push it back again. Breathe deep, love, deep as you can.* Again the light rushed against the swelling, and Féolan thought, ridiculously, of a mountain ram, crashing headlong against his opponent to claim his ewe. My stubborn Human, he thought, and then cast thought aside and sucked at the glorious air like a greedy baby, as deep into his lungs as he could.

And then she was gone from him, and he was back in the desert, stumbling into the eternal night.

CHAPTER THIRTY-FOUR

GABRIELLE RUMMAGED FRANTICALLY in her kit. Féolan's life was measured now in heartbeats. The Veil extended right back to his windpipe and the surrounding tissues, saturated with poison, had swelled together into a solid wall. It had taken every bit of her power to open the brief cracks that allowed Féolan to win a couple of breaths. Even fresh, she could not have held back that mass of flesh and accomplished the healing that would open his airways again. And she was far from fresh.

She chose hurriedly from among her bonemender's blades and pulled out the glass pipette used to measure out drops of medicine. It was far too narrow, but it was all she had at hand.

"Derkh, do you see this glass tube?" she asked. She did not look at him but prepared Féolan as she spoke, rolling up a blanket and placing it under his neck so that his head tipped back and the bump known as the baby's fist protruded. "I need something like this, only bigger around. Glass or metal, even wood at need." At home, the delicate neck of a wine bottle, broken off at the base, would serve. But Tarzine wine was stored in jugs with short, broad mouths. She could think of nothing to suggest to Derkh.

It was Dominic, who had stuck his head in the door just moments earlier, who replied.

"I can get it."

"Okay." There was no time for thanks or further instructions.

"Then, Derkh, you can help me here. I need the dropper end of this pipette broken off."

She turned to Féolan. His lips were blue, hands twitching weakly. His eyes stared unseeing. She must act now or give him up for dead.

Her fingers found the bottom ridge of his baby's fist. She laid the tip of her knife against the indentation directly beneath it and cut in to the second mark on the blade—about from her fingertip to her first joint. She pinched the ends of the incision toward each other so that the wound gaped open and heard the fleeting sucking gasp as air found its way into Féolan's windpipe.

"Derkh?"

The pipette he laid into her hand was not jagged shards at one end, as she had feared, but finished with a clean sharp break. She hadn't seen him score around the end with his knife and tap it sharply over the table edge. She was just glad she had given the job to a jewelry maker.

"That's perfect. Thank you." Gabrielle tucked the smooth end of the pipette into the opening she had made in Féolan's windpipe. She put her lips around the cut end and blew.

She heard Derkh's excited exclamation as Féolan's chest rose with her breath. It was so little, though, the stream of air she could send through the narrow pipette. There was no way it would sustain him without the extra force of a person blowing into it. She counted a slow three and blew again. One–two–three. Again. Beside her, Derkh dabbed with a towel at the blood that had spilled. There wasn't much from this sort of incision—not to her bonemender's eyes at least. It probably seemed a lot to Derkh.

She kept up the steady rhythm, and felt Féolan flutter back to consciousness. He would be awake when she had to widen the incision for the new tube. And he was still so sick—she had only bought him a little time, not healed anything.

Fear and exhaustion welled up, and she found her throat so choked and tight that her breath drew in with a noisy ragged gasp. She shook off the tears, furious, and bent to the tube to blow. She couldn't. Her breath escaped in useless sobs that gasped out around the pipette. Oh, Great Mother. She would kill him if she didn't get hold of herself.

Derkh's hand squeezed her shoulder, coaxing her aside. "I can do this for a while."

She let him take her place at Féolan's side, relief and gratitude bringing more tears. She sat on the floor, rocking with the ship as the freshening dawn breeze gusted at the sails, and wept.

SHE WAS CRYING still, though softly, the tension that had stretched her nerves tight as *lythra* strings eased by the tears, when Dominic returned. He stopped just inside the door, confused by the scene before him: the blood, Derkh bent over Féolan, Gabrielle in tears on the floor...

"Is he...?"

Derkh shook his head. "He's hanging on."

"Then why...?" Dominic cut his eyes toward his sister. He had seen her work many times, always calm, in charge, unflappable.

Derkh's reply was sharp. "She's been up for two days straight without a break. She worked right through the night on your daughter." He paused to blow once more into the glass tube. "It drains her. It's like she pours her own life into her patient." Derkh was surprised Gabrielle's own brother didn't know this. He had learned it first-hand, when Gabrielle, still a complete stranger, had worked herself to the point of collapse to save his life.

"I'm not so drained I don't hear you talking about me." Gabrielle wiped her eyes and stood up. She stretched out her back and neck, squared her shoulders, and the weepy overwhelmed woman disappeared. She was, once more, the healer.

"Did you find anything?"

Dominic held up a copper whistle. About a hand-span long, it was used by the Tarzines to give orders that could carry from one end of the ship to the other.

Gabrielle took it in her palm and considered. Copper was soft—Derkh could probably cut off the end with the mouthpiece and holes in short order, and the remaining length was about right. But if the pipette was too narrow, this was really too wide. Féolan would be able to breathe through it freely, once he got the knack, but Gabrielle would have to cut into his vocal cords to make room. The damage from the scarring could be permanent.

It would have to do. She took over at the pipette and sent Derkh to saw off the whistle. "Clean it up as best you can too," she added. The inside would be coated with the spit from who knew how many Tarzine sailors.

FÉOLAN HOVERED AT the edge of consciousness, unable to speak, his thoughts wheeling and floating with the fever. His throat was blocked tight, yet somehow air came—though never quite enough—to his lungs. Pain ate at him. He was sickening everywhere at once: the Veil had sent tendrils twining through his body, and they fastened like leeches and sucked away his life.

Gabrielle was back. He heard her voice in his mind, tried to follow her words. She was apologizing for something. Not saving him, he supposed. *It's all right, love.* He was ready to die. Or rather, he was tired of trying to live. Tired of the pain, tired of starving for air, tired above all of fighting the terror that made him want to scream and claw for breath.

The cut that she made seared into his neck. The Veil has made me deaf, he thought wildly, for he could not hear his own cry of pain. But the pain abated, and sweet air came flooding into him, free and ungrudging, his lungs gulping it in of their own accord without any direction from him. He was momentarily drunk with it, the air rushing to his head like strong wine. I'll die happy now, he thought, his own voice a giddy babble in his mind, and drink air for all eternity.

DOMINIC RETURNED WITH breakfast, and he and Derkh each stationed themselves at a bedside while Gabrielle ate. Madeleine was awake, weak but clear-eyed and lucid, able to sip at the tea Dominic had brought and nibble at the fruit. She reached up to wipe away the tears that tracked down her father's cheeks, and he caught up her hand and held it tight, kissing the palm. They grinned at each other foolishly, though Dominic felt a twinge of guilt at his happiness. He was worried and sorry for Féolan and his sister, but his daughter lived, and he could not stay his gladness.

Derkh watched Féolan and Gabrielle with equal watchfulness. Féolan lay with a copper pipe protruding from the middle of his neck, the pale skin streaked with blood that had run back into his dark hair. He was shockingly pale—the phrase "deathly white" came to Derkh and he shoved it angrily from his mind. The gray luminous eyes glittered under half-open lids. Féolan's chest heaved and fell—he was, indeed, breathing through Gabrielle's tube—but Derkh didn't think he would have the strength to haul air from this strange well much longer.

And Gabrielle? Her drawn face and shadowed eyes betrayed her fatigue. She ate steadily, mechanically, not tasting the food but merely taking it in. Like feeding a woodstove, he thought, remembering the great ovens in Castle DesChênes where bread and pastries were baked. He had fed those ovens on occasion, felt their roaring blind hunger.

He waited until she was done and had drained her water mug.

"Gabrielle?" She glanced at him, too weary perhaps to respond with words. But then the smudged eyes sparked with warmth, and she managed a small but genuine smile.

"Thank you for your help," she said. "I don't know how—"

He waved it off. "Can you rest a little now? I can wake you if—"

She shook her head. "We are already at the 'if.' Féolan has one chance to live, and it's now."

Derkh nodded soberly. "I feared as much. Can I do anything to help you?"

She was climbing into the narrow bed, burrowing in between Féolan and the wall. "I'm going to work until sleep takes me. Another blanket would be nice, over both of us. And make sure his breathing tube stays free."

Gabrielle closed her eyes. Derkh watched for a bit, filled with the memory of the long hours Gabrielle had spent healing him. It was a wonder to him still, the mystery of her power.

CHAPTER THIRTY-FIVE

FÉOLAN OPENED HIS EYES and knew that he would live. Gabrielle slept beside him—for more than two days, she had done nothing but flood her light into him and sleep like a dead woman. Féolan did not know how much time had passed, knew only that she had been a constant presence in his heart and mind, that she had sent a light blasting after him more than once when he had wandered into utter darkness. Only for the last half-day or so did he have any coherent sense of time or reliable memory. That was when the illness finally loosed its grip enough that he could perceive what she was doing and rally some strength to help her.

She had dammed up the leakage of poison into his system, and when at last the seeping stopped, the reactive swelling in his throat began to diminish. Yet she left the tube in place, though the irritation of it had become a trial, and the membrane as well. Instead she was sending her light to places where the poison concentration was most dangerous. Bit by bit, she labored to clear his heart, kidneys and eyes and to undo the damage that had begun there. The tube, the thick ugly growth in his throat: these were minor discomforts by comparison, and Féolan tried to bear them patiently.

Féolan woke and slept; the stuffy cramped room grew dark and brightened; the seas rocked soothingly or slammed against the ship. People came and went, bringing food for Gabrielle or visiting Madeleine. Often Derkh sat near him. Gabrielle sometimes slept in a hammock Dominic had scrounged and strung across the middle of the cabin.

At last the day came when Gabrielle told him she was going to remove the Veil. She helped him to his elbows and knees, so his head was lowered. "I don't want it to fall in and choke you," she said.

He felt her light fill his throat, felt the thick scabby growth slough away like a horny snakeskin. It filled the back of his mouth, nauseating him, and he felt a rising panic, unable with the paralysis that still slowed his tongue to move it forward.

"Cough," commanded Gabrielle, and even as his mind protested that he could not, not with a hole gaping into his windpipe, her hand snaked around and covered the exposed end. "Now."

It was a feeble uncoordinated effort, but enough. Féolan fished frantically in his mouth, and pulled out a tongue of mottled gray-black flesh nearly as long as the palm of his hand. It lay on the towel Gabrielle had provided like a strip of rotted boot leather, and Féolan recoiled at the putrid reek of the thing. Panting with exertion from this small adventure—through mouth and whistling copper tubing both at once—he lay back onto his side.

"Feels good, doesn't it?"

Féolan looked across the cabin to find Madeleine sitting up in bed, watching them. She grinned, and he smiled and nodded. It did feel good. Madeleine was thin from days without food but clearly on the mend. Her smile dissolved into troubled seriousness.

"Féolan, I'm really sorry I made you sick."

He hoisted up on one elbow and shook his head, wishing he could speak to her. Tried to think what gesture a Human girl would understand. He pointed to Madeleine, cupped his hand close to his chest as if it held a baby bird or precious gift, then laid the hand over his heart.

Madeleine's eyes filled with tears, but her trembly smile was brilliant. She understood.

GABRIELLE GAVE THE tube a sharp twist, murmuring an apology at Féolan's grimace, and eased it out. She laid her hand flat over the gaping flap of skin.

"Try a breath?"

She felt suction on her palm, but Féolan's breath flowed easily through his nostrils. He smiled, but she didn't return it. She had bad news to tell him.

"Love, the incision in your skin will heal fine. You'll have a little scar, but it won't feel any different from before."

He nodded, eyebrows raised questioningly. *Then why the frown?*

"The problem is with your vocal cords. I had to cut into them, and they have already scarred over along the cut edges. I wasn't able to prevent it because—well, I was kind of busy trying to keep you alive." Another nod. "The thing is, I can't do much with scar tissue. It's healthy flesh, but in some ways it acts dead. It's like—" She groped for an analogy. "Like trying to make a stone grow.

"Scarring is a good way to heal skin, but it's stiff and it's going to keep your vocal cords from working properly. Your voice is going to be—I'm not really sure. You'll be able to speak all right, but you might sound hoarse and raspy."

Like a Human, he joked, speaking directly to her mind. It won only a fleeting smile.

"Maybe eventually, after I've worked to stretch out the scar to give it more flexibility, and you have learned to work with just the undamaged part of your voice. At first, maybe more like a cross between a man and a raven."

No more singing.

"Probably not in public," she acknowledged. She waited while he digested this information before offering an alternative. It was not the course she would recommend, but it was his decision to make.

"The only way to undo the damage would be to cut away the scar tissue and control the healing over the next few days. I'll do it if you want me to, but I have to tell you it will be painful, and difficult to do properly."

He was already shaking his head. *I'm alive. It's enough.*

Thank the gods, Gabrielle thought, and her smile shone down at him, full of love and admiration. It would be hard for an Elf, she knew, to be unable to sing. But it would have been hard for her to cut into him again for any but the most pressing need.

"You're sure?" she asked, needing to know she had not pressed her wishes upon him. He nodded.

"I'll just put a patch over this incision then, so you can breathe easier and learn to speak again while it heals."

She was proud of the ingenuity of the patch she had designed. She had boiled clean a length of sausage casing from the galley stores and cut out a double thickness for strength. Stuck on with a generous layer of gum mastic, it made a smooth, thin, flexible seal.

She took a moment to admire her handiwork and another moment to look over her patient. The eyes that gazed back at her were no longer those of an invalid. They were once again the deep dancing eyes of her true love, and what lay in their brilliant depths brought the blood up to her cheeks.

"Your eyes are feeling better, I see," she said tartly. Her smile betrayed her, though—she could not keep the corners severely straight no matter how hard she thought serious thoughts.

"Much." The word was a breathy whisper, his first awkward and uncomfortable attempt at speech.

"Shhhhh." Gabrielle put her finger to his lips to emphasize her command. "Let your poor neck relax for a while before hurting it with sounds." And to ensure he obeyed, she took her finger out of the way and kissed him.

MATTHIEU WAS SO restless he felt he might crawl out of his own skin. There was nothing to do on the ship but get in the way and no one to do it with. His dad spent hours every day in the sick room, attending to Maddy. Matthieu didn't begrudge it, and he just about lived for the little time every afternoon that Madeleine was allowed to come out on deck, but it made for a long lonely day.

He was allowed to visit the sick room now, and he did, but it was stuffy and crowded, full of grown-ups, and without a chiggers board or set of counters, there was nothing to do there either but sit on a chair beside Madeleine and try to think of something to say.

She had thanked him for looking after her when she was first sick, but neither of them was ready to talk about their time as captives. Luc's death waited there. Yet what else was there to talk about? The weather? The food? Grandma Solange's birthday party? It all seemed silly and forced.

Too bad you couldn't lay out *reneñas* tiles on bedclothes. Yolenka, seeing Matthieu's boredom, had pulled him aside about a week ago and taught him to play. Matthieu had enjoyed the game immensely, and Yolenka had laughed and called him a "born gambler." She had played with him a couple of times since, but he didn't feel he could pester her for more.

Matthieu wandered to the bow of the ship and wedged himself into the lookout. The narrow triangular space at the very end of the outthrust prow was used by the Tarzines in uncertain waters, but was vacant now. Matthieu lay on his stomach and pushed his head under the safety ropes, so that he was looking straight down into green ocean. The rushing of the ship against the waves was loud in his ears, while above his head the little sail that stretched out to the tip of the long bowsprit snapped in the brisk wind. The ship rose and fell on the swell, each new surge soaking his face with salt spray. It was hypnotic and slightly scary all at once, and for the first time in days Matthieu was utterly absorbed. He wiggled forward a little more, trying to look back under the bow to the spot where the keel sank into the sea.

Three whistle blasts interrupted him—that meant it was almost dinnertime, for the passengers and whatever crew members were off duty. Dinner wasn't much to look forward to after two weeks at sea. Surely they must be close to home by now. He raised his head to scan the horizon. Maybe he would be the first to spot land.

No land, but…he craned his neck to the left, trying to hold

the place where something had caught his eye just as the ship dipped into a trough. The ship rose and—

It was sails. Ochre-yellow sails, lit up in the rays of the late afternoon sun.

Blood pounded in his ears, his heart became a fist battering at the cage of his ribs.

"Pirates!" he yelled. His voice was caught in the wind and spray and swallowed up. He tried to scramble to his feet, clipped the back of his head on the safety rope and wiggled backward, clothes and hair dripping onto the deck. Standing, he shaded his face and squinted into the sun. Where were they?

Matthieu climbed onto the second rope rail, steadying himself on the sturdy lines that anchored the forward sail to the deck. His eyes scanned feverishly.

Yes, there—it ran before the wind, bearing toward them like a great malevolent falcon.

No one heard him, or even paid him any mind. He would have to grab the nearest sailor and make him see.

Matthieu lifted his foot to step down to the deck. The ship yawed in a sudden side-swell. The rope in his hand went slack as the sail swung. He fell forward over the rail with nothing to counterbalance against.

With a lurch, the ship righted itself, and the sail rope snapped tight. But Matthieu could not hang on. Like the last child in a whip-snap game, he was flung off into the sea.

CHAPTER THIRTY-SIX

THE CAPTAIN OF THE TARZINE SHIP passed the spyglass over to his lord. The prince widened his stance, bracing himself against the roll of the ship, and squinted through the narrow eyepiece.

"That's him! We have them. Captain, are we on course to intercept?"

"Nearly. Just a slight adjustment."

"Good. Go ahead and adjust our course."

The captain turned away to convey these orders, but a startled cry from the prince pulled him back.

"He's fallen overboard! Devils of the deep! I don't think anyone has seen him."

The prince lowered the spyglass and shouted at the captain. "What are you standing here for? Get over there, with all speed you can make, before he drowns in plain sight!" He clapped the glass back to his eye and stared over the waves.

THE OCEAN WAS shockingly cold and far rougher than it seemed from high above on deck. Matthieu was tossed and tumbled as he plunged into the water, the wake from the ship pushing him one way and the oncoming waves another. He managed to hold his breath, though, and when he finally surfaced he was glad that the turbulence had at least tossed him clear of the ship—he had feared being crushed or suffocated beneath the great hull.

But it was such a long way up to the deck, and the crew were distracted by the change of shift and the dinner whistle.

Matthieu tried his best to yell for help, using the moments when the waves receded and he was in least danger of swallowing a faceful of seawater. He yelled and screamed, trying with growing despair to make his voice carry over the wind and cut through the racket of the ship itself. Yet she pulled steadily away, and the merciless sea widened between them. He was lost.

Impossible. It was impossible. His father could not have traveled so far to find him, only for Matthieu to die so stupidly, so close to home.

The water dragged and sucked at him as he treaded water, pulling on his legs, arcing heavy sheets of water over his head. He was so tired already. He tried, between strokes and waves, to kick off his boots. The one floated away easily, leaving his foot light and free. He mistimed the other and got a choking mouthful of salt for his mistake.

He struggled to cough it out, and another wave broke over his head. This is how people drown, he thought. One little mistake after another. One boy against an endless ocean of waves; it was hopeless.

When Matthieu saw the yellow sails looming against the sky, he thought at first that he'd got turned around and it was his father's ship come back for him. Elation surged in his heart.

But of course it was not his ship. It was the pirates coming after him. Coming to reclaim their plunder.

He wept now, wept with fear and rage, the tears hidden in the seawater that streamed down his face, sobs choked out around the chop of the waves. They were coming for him, and he would go to them. He would go, because he didn't have the courage to let the waves take him. He would be taken back to the Tarzine lands, and he would be all alone.

STRONG HANDS REACHED out to him, caught first at his billowing shirt and then his arms. He was hauled into a dinghy, gasping and dizzy, black flares in front of his eyes. His belly roiled and he vomited in great coughing convulsions, stomach and lungs both ridding themselves of what felt like pails full of seawater.

Someone was holding his shoulders as he retched, steadying him. When he was done, they wrapped around his chest and hauled him backward, pulling him against a broad warm body. Matthieu tried to fight, weak as he was. He mumbled curses and pulled against the arms that held him. Let them cut his throat for it, what difference did it make?

Then the voice that had been speaking quietly in his ear penetrated.

"Matthieu. Easy, son. Easy. You're safe now, lad. Matthieu, it's me."

Matthieu twisted around to stare at his captor. Thick blond hair whipping in the wind. Blue eyes that twinkled when they teased. A mouth that was almost always smiling—but not now. Now it looked, just a little, like it might be crying.

Matthieu flung himself into his uncle Tristan's waiting arms and held on tight.

DOMINIC'S SHIP SAILED into Blanchette harbor early the next afternoon with a full escort from Tristan's new sea patrol: two tubby Krylian merchant vessels and the Tarzine pirate ship they had managed to capture during a raid.

Tristan grinned at Dominic's surprise. "You didn't think I'd be sitting around here doing nothing while you were gone? I would have lost my mind worrying about you and driven Rosie to distraction."

"You did drive me to distraction," Rosalie retorted, "but it made no difference—we were all crazy with worry anyway."

"It is one of Turga's ships, I hope?" asked Yolenka. Tristan shrugged.

"Haven't been able to find out yet—we need an interpreter. Actually, I was wondering if you—"

"I am yours." Yolenka offered herself with a dancer's courtesy.

"Hang on. I thought you said you were mine!" Derkh objected. His dark eyebrows drew down in displeasure.

"Derkh, I mean only…Is not—" Yolenka discomfited was a rare sight, and Derkh enjoyed it. Briefly. Then he relented.

"I'm joking. You're not the only one who can act a part."

Dominic hooted with laughter. Tristan and Rosie looked bemused.

"If you had seen what this man suffered," Dominic explained. "He deserves his revenge."

"What I do, I do for your children!" Yolenka rounded on him, color rising into her golden cheeks.

"I know it." Dominic became serious. "Yolenka, I know it, and I want to thank you again. You were magnificent—your dancing and everything else."

White teeth flashed into brilliance. Yolenka turned to Derkh, her smile triumphant.

"You see? Here is man who understands art."

Matthieu and Madeleine were alone at last. The entire DesChênes clan had met their ship at the pier; but Justine and Solange had spirited the two children straight home. There they had been embraced, exclaimed at and wept over, bathed and fed and dosed with "strengthening tonic," hugged first shyly and then with exuberant glee by Sylvain, questioned and sometimes just stared at with silent hunger by their mother. They had borne it all patiently, happily even.

Now, as Sylvain commandeered his grandmother's attention and Justine, satisfied at last that her children really were all right, pulled herself away to catch up with Dominic, their eyes met. The smile that passed between them was complicated: a shared acknowledgement that it was good, better than good, to be home—and that home was not quite the same. *They* were not quite the same.

Neither had any doubt that they would soon be bickering and annoying each other just like before. But they knew now that the bond between them was stronger than any bickering. What they had been through together, how they had stood by each other—that was forever.

The afternoon sun streamed through the sunroom's skylight, brightening every corner and setting fire to Madeleine's hair.

"So, Matthieu," she said.

Her smile grew into a challenging grin.

"Want to play chiggers?"

EPILOGUE

THE FIRST LASTING SNOWFALL of the year powdered the tree branches and muffled their footsteps. Gabrielle walked lightly, enjoying the glittering silent woodland. Winter would bring hardship to many: dwindling food stores, freezing nights, coughs and illnesses of all kinds. Yet in winter's first weeks, she couldn't help loving the swaddled mysterious beauty of a world blanketed in snow.

Féolan led the way, slipping through the branches as soundlessly as a ghost. Gabrielle had improved, but she would never match the Elves' ability to glide through deep woods with hardly a rustle. He must be nervous, Gabrielle thought, to come so far into the forest. He needs to be sure no one will overhear.

At last, in the protected circle of a small clearing, he brushed off a fallen log, sat her down and stood before her. He seemed about to speak, searching for words, but then he shrugged. "Ah, it is what it is. I'm just stalling." And he opened his mouth and began to sing.

He chose a cradlesong, simpler in its melody than most Elvish music but beautiful and hypnotic.

Gabrielle closed her eyes to listen, not wanting to be distracted by Féolan's self-consciousness or to increase it by staring.

It was certainly not the clear fluid voice she was used to.

The voice that sang to her now was deeper, with a distinct grain. Growly in the bottom notes and husky at the top of his range, Féolan's voice was like no other Elf's on earth. Yet the more she listened, the more Gabrielle heard warmth and depth and Féolan's own sure musicality. He had found the beauty in the damaged instrument he had been given.

The song came to an end, but Gabrielle sat still, holding the sound in her mind.

Féolan cleared his throat. "That bad?"

"Oh, love, no, I'm sorry!" Gabrielle was penitent. "That was mean, to keep you waiting while I daydreamed."

He shifted his weight, like a boy at lessons asked to recite. "What do you think, then?"

She grinned at him. "Well, you'll never be asked to sing at a wedding or baby naming."

He laughed in agreement, the tension broken. Eyed her. "Is there a 'but' to come?"

"There is indeed," she agreed. "BUT—I know of at least two people who will always be glad to listen to you sing."

"You being one?"

"Me being one," she said. She kept him waiting just for a heartbeat. "Your child being the other."

"My—"

Gabrielle watched as the import of her words took hold. She had never seen his eyes so round.

"Are you sure?" he asked. "So soon?"

"So soon?" Now it was her turn to stare. "It's been six years!"

"That's what I mean," he began. Then he closed his mouth.

Walked over to her, pulled her up from her log and wrapped her in his arms.

"Even after six years, now and then our worlds bump together, and I am slow to catch on," he said. "It wasn't soon for you, was it?"

She shook her head against his chest, a little teary. "I was wondering if it would ever happen."

They held each other in the snowy silent clearing. Then Gabrielle pulled back a little. "I'm sorry to take you by surprise. Will it be a problem?"

"It will be wonderful." He meant it. Had she been blindfolded and missed the dazed silly grin that spread across his face, she would still have felt his delight. "Some surprises are good. Some are wonderful."

"Féolan, I'm afraid I lied to you earlier," Gabrielle confessed. "You *will* be asked to sing at a baby naming, after all."

Holly Bennett is the author of *The Bonemender* and *The Bonemender's Oath,* prequels to *The Bonemender's Choice,* as well as the Druidic fantasy, *The Warrior's Daughter.* In addition to writing, she is editor-in-chief of *Today's Parent* Special Editions. Born in Montreal, Quebec, she lives in Peterborough, Ontario, with a houseful of musicians (three sons and a husband) and a nice quiet dog.

New York Public Library Books for the Teen Age
IRA Notable Book
Canadian Children's Book Centre Our Choice starred selection
Ontario Library Association White Pine Award nominee

The Bonemender
978-1-55143-336-3 $9.95 CDN • $8.95 US PB
Ages 12+

"...will appeal to fantasy and adventure fans alike." —*KLIATT*

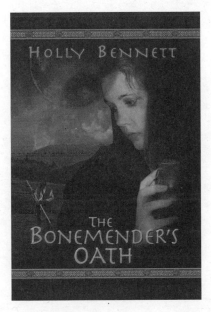

The Bonemender's Oath
978-1-55143-443-8 $9.95 CDN • $8.95 US PB
Ages 12+

"...engaging characters, suspense, a subtle dose of humor and wonderfully descriptive tones...with strong ties to honor, love, family and friendship."

—*KLIATT*

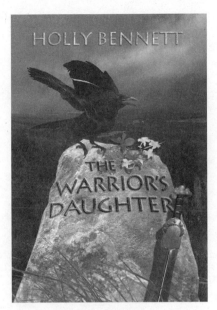

The Warrior's Daughter
978-1-55143-607-4 $9.95 CDN • $8.95 US PB
Ages 12+

"...told with insight, compassion and skill...Bennett becomes, book by book, an ever more accomplished writer of fantasy..."

—*Okanagan College Deakin Newsletter*